William H. Venable, George Gordon Byron

Selections from the Poems of Lord Byron

William H. Venable, George Gordon Byron

Selections from the Poems of Lord Byron

ISBN/EAN: 9783337483630

Printed in Europe, USA, Canada, Australia, Japan

Cover: Foto ©Andreas Hilbeck / pixelio.de

More available books at **www.hansebooks.com**

ECLECTIC ENGLISH CLASSICS

SELECTIONS
FROM THE POEMS OF
LORD BYRON

EDITED BY W. H. VENABLE, LL.D.

OF THE WALNUT HILLS HIGH SCHOOL, CINCINNATI

NEW YORK ·∶· CINCINNATI ·∶· CHICAGO

AMERICAN BOOK COMPANY

1898

2466

CONTENTS.

INTRODUCTION.

GEORGE GORDON, LORD BYRON, born of unruly blood in a revolutionary age, was destined to lead revolutionary movements in both the political and the literary world. His ancestry, though noble, had in it a fierce, ungovernable strain. His adventurous grandfather, or, as Byron called him in verse, "granddad," was known to fame as "Foul-weather Jack;" his father, "a handsome rake," bore the nickname of "Mad Jack;" and the poet's uncle, who in a fit of rage killed a neighbor, was distinguished as the "Wicked Byron." Lord Byron's mother was vain, violent, passionate, yet fond,—an hysterical woman whose character was a mixture of strength and weakness. She was of Scotch birth, with some blood royal of the Stuart family in her proud veins. Her maiden name was Gordon.

"Mad Jack" Byron deserted his wife soon after the birth of their only child, George, who first saw the light in 1788, in the city of London. The abandoned mother removed with her child to Aberdeen, Scotland, where they resided about ten years, until, by the death of the "Wicked Byron," the boy inherited the title of baron and the large estates and feudal hall of Newstead Abbey.

Though "Geordie" was sent to school irregularly, at Aberdeen

7

and elsewhere, his education was really neglected, and he learned neither to study nor to obey, but grew up a typical spoiled child. He did, indeed, get some lessons from the lofty mountain, "dark Lochnagar." On becoming a young lord, he was put under the care of a guardian, Lord Carlisle, who placed him in the public school of Harrow. The head master of this celebrated boys' school soon discovered in the thirteen-year-old lad "a wild mountain colt; but *there was mind in his eye.*" The energy of Byron's mind in his school and college days was given more to general reading than to systematic study. It is recorded that he was a poor penman and disliked mathematics, but acquired a fair knowledge of the classics, some French, and much Italian. His mastery of bodily accomplishments was admirable, considering the disadvantage he suffered from a deformity in his right foot, causing a slight lameness. Notwithstanding this defect, Byron was a skillful a hlete,—could ride, row, swim, box, fence, and shoot better than most of his comrades. He shrank from the sports of the chase, not from timidity,—for his pets were dogs, bears, and wolves,—but because he hated all forms of cruelty. He was not a bully, neither would he be imposed upon, and he never could understand the submissive spirit. With true Scotch-English pluck, he fought his way from misery to victory, and this explains his saying: "I hated Harrow till the last year and a half, but then I liked it."

From Harrow he went to Trinity College, Cambridge, against his wish, for he wanted to go to Oxford. He was now a youth of seventeen, and his turbulent soul began to seek vent for its emotions in verse. A poet born, he wrote easily, naturally; and the book he published in his nineteenth year, prettily called "Hours of Idleness," had in it as much thought and sentiment as the author had thus far experienced in real life. He took his degree in 1808, and went to London.

His first poems were written for pleasure and from the stirrings of boyish ambition to win a name. His second venture had a very different motive and temper. The " Hours of Idleness " was severely criticised in the " Edinburgh Review," and Byron struck back fiercely in a satire called " English Bards and Scotch Reviewers," beginning with the audacious lines:

> " Prepare for rime : I'll publish, right or wrong;
> Fools are my theme, let satire be my song."

The author afterwards saw that there was much more wrong than right in this literary challenge.

The year after he left college, Byron made his first tour of the Continent, traveling two years in Spain, Albania, and Greece. On his return to England early in 1812, he published the first two cantos of " Childe Harold," a poem that was immediately recognized, even by his enemies, as a work of genius, though the poet himself was not aware of its excellence. Surprised at his own success, he wrote: " I awoke one morning and found myself famous." His poetry stirred the heart of Europe. It thrilled London like an electric shock. Byron, upon whom the Muse had bestowed a new lordship, was idolized by society. About four years of his life were spent in London and at Newstead Abbey, devoted to the excitements of fashionable life, the dissipations of pleasure, and the solace of literary composition. It was in this period of conventional distinction that he wooed and won Miss Milbanke, who became Lady Byron in January, 1815.

The marriage, being one of convenience, not of love on either side, proved unhappy. Byron had many love affairs, none of them fortunate.   It is truly said by one of his biographers, " He was the slave and the despot of women, their adorer and their contemner."   Only a year elapsed from the time she became his wife until Lady Byron left her husband, taking with her their infant daughter.   Byron said the causes of the separation were too simple to be explained, and they have never been explained to the satisfaction of the world.

Byron was violently blamed in England, not only for his treatment of his wife, but for general dissolute conduct and for the audacity of his sentiments.   Such was the revulsion of public feeling, so vehement was the outcry against him, that, as he afterwards wrote, he felt that if what was said were true he was unfit for England; if false, England was unfit for him.   Under the circumstances his pride dictated but one course: on the 25th of April, 1816, he quitted England, never to return.   Only four years of his mature life had been passed in his native land.   He was but twenty-eight years old when he set out on his second and final visit to southern Europe.

He went in a rage against mankind.   Now he had knowledge of life, good and bad, and now there was something real of which to write.   He traveled in Switzerland and Italy, seeing all things vividly, thinking intensely, feeling profoundly, and pouring out his whole mind in eloquent verse.   Never poet wrote more rapidly.   By far the best of his poems were produced in Italy.   At length, after six or seven years of varied experience, not free from licentiousness, he seemed to tire of himself, to weary of sensual delights, and even to lose interest in the poetic art.

Political questions called his energies away from poetry to war.   An ardent lover of liberty, he wished to promote the actual freedom of oppressed nations.   Not content to sing the imaginary song of a Greek bard, he felt a noble longing to aid with his money and his sword the Greek people in their struggle against the Turk. On the 4th of July, 1823, he sailed from Genoa to Greece, to join in an expedition against Lepanto. He was put in command of a division of troops, but did not live to lead it to battle. The great poet died of a fever at Missolonghi, three months after having completed his thirty-sixth year. His last words, spoken in delirium, were true to his nature: "Forward, forward! Follow me. Do not be afraid." Thus died the poet whose pen was a sword, and whose sword was as brave as his pen.

Byron's political influence was considerable. Born just after the American Revolution, and just before the French, he breathed the quick atmosphere of his age. We may call him an aristocratic democrat. In theory he was one of the people. He admired Washington and American institutions. "Give me a republic," he said when about to aid the Greek revolutionists. An English author calls him "the greatest modern preacher of 'liberty, equality, and fraternity.'"

But literature, not politics, was the realm in which his chief influence was exerted. Minto pronounces Byron "the greatest literary force of this century." Matthew Arnold, a cautious critic, says: "His name is still great and brilliant. Wordsworth and Byron stand out by themselves." In France and Germany Byron is greatly admired. In the United States he has ever been appreciated. He wrote of Daniel Boone and the West, and was proud of his audience in the Ohio Valley. "This is the first tidings that has sounded to me like fame,—to be redde on the banks of the Ohio," he wrote in his diary in 1813.

Byron's poetry is by no means free from faults. It violates many rules of versification, and even of rhetoric and grammar.

Nevertheless it takes high rank. Byron's poetry is Byron, his life, his passions,—an expression of superabundant energy, like his loves, his hatreds, his sports, his military enterprise. As fast as he lived he transmuted his life into written song. Every event gave rise to a lyric, a romance, or a drama. One critic thinks force and sincerity are the chief elements of Byron's poetry; another says the main constituents are passion and wit. As for his style, at the best, perhaps no one has described it more happily than Swinburne, who says it is "at once swift and supple, light and strong, various and radiant."

The selections in this book give a fair idea of Byron's genius and art. The first, "The Prisoner of Chillon," is an old favorite, not without cause. Though not in the author's usual vein, it shows his character in its gentlest and most serious mood. The piece was written at Ouchy, near Geneva, in two days, June 26, 27, 1816. It is one of the best of Byron's romantic "tales,"—a species of poem made popular by Scott, who ceased to produce such because, as he said, "Byron *beat* me."

From "Childe Harold's Pilgrimage" we give by far the best portion, Cantos III. and IV., the former describing Belgium and Switzerland, the latter Italy. The third canto was finished June 27, 1816, and went to press early in 1817. The fourth was begun in June, 1817, completed in December of the same year, and published in 1818. Aside from their literary merit, these cantos possess high educational value, especially to the student of the classics, because they afford a delightful opportunity to review history and mythology and to impress important facts of topography, biography, literature, and art. Discussing the poetical worth of these cantos, Professor Nichol uses these strong words:

" Cantos III. and IV. are separated from their predecessors, not by a stage, but by a gulf. Previous to their publication Byron had only shown how far the force of rhapsody could go ; now he struck with his right hand and from the shoulder." A still subtler critic, Swinburne, after praising the concluding stanzas of the fourth canto, the apostrophe to the ocean, says discriminately : " No other passage in the fourth canto will bear to be torn out from the text ; and this one suffers by extraction. The other three cantos are more loosely built and less compact of fabric ; but in the first two there is little to remember or to praise."

The text followed in these selections is that of the Oxford edition from the Oxford University Press, which is based upon the standard Murray edition. The notes, it is hoped, will not seem too many to the teacher nor too few for the independent student. The editor has made use of the researches of H. F. Tozer (Clarendon Press Series), of H. G. Keene (Bell's Classics), and of the American scholar, W. J. Rolfe, by permission.

Only one pedagogical hint is here ventured, alike to teacher and to pupil : avoid, in teaching or learning English poetry, the danger pointed out by Byron in Stanzas LXXV.–LXXVII. of Canto IV., "Childe Harold." May the young reader both " comprehend " and " love " the verse.

LIST OF BYRON'S WORKS.

MISCELLANEOUS:

Hours of Idleness (72 titles); Occasional Pieces (82 titles); Hebrew Melodies (23 titles); Domestic Pieces (63 titles); — in all 240 poems, among which are many beautiful lyrics.

SATIRES:

English Bards and Scotch Reviewers; Hints from Horace; The Curse of Minerva; The Waltz; The Age of Bronze; The Blues: A Literary Eclogue; The Vision of Judgment.

TALES:

The Giaour; The Bride of Abydos; The Corsair; Lara; The Siege of Corinth; Parisina; The Prisoner of Chillon; Mazeppa; The Island; Beppo.

DRAMAS:

Manfred; Marino Faliero; Sardanapalus; The Two Foscari; Cain; Heaven and Earth; Werner; The Deformed Transformed.

UNCLASSIFIED:

Childe Harold's Pilgrimage; Don Juan; The Lament of Tasso; The Prophecy of Dante; The Morgante Maggiore of Pulci; Francesca of Rimini.

Some of the best of the longer poems, regarded from a literary standpoint, are " The Giaour," " Manfred," " Cain," "The Vision of Judgment," " Beppo," and " Don Juan." Of course "The Prisoner of Chillon " and " Childe Harold ' are considered masterpieces.

CHRONOLOGICAL OUTLINE OF BYRON'S LIFE.

YEAR	EVENT	BYRON'S AGE

1788, January 22. Byron was born in London.

1798. Byron inherited his title and estate. 10

1801. Entered the boys' school at Harrow 13

1805. Entered Trinity College, Cambridge 17

1807. Published his "Hours of Idleness" 19

1809, July. Sailed for the Continent 21

1809 to 1811, July. Traveled in Spain, Greece, etc.

1812, February. Made his first speech in the House of
    Lords; published "Childe Harold," Cantos I. and II. 24

1812 to 1816. Was lionized in England.

1815, January. Married Miss Milbanke 27

1816, January. His wife separated from him 28

1816, April 25. Byron left England, never to return. .

1816 to 1823, July. Resided in Switzerland and in Italy.

1823, July 4. Sailed from Genoa for Greece. 35

1824, April 19. Died at Missolonghi 36

THE PRISONER OF CHILLON.

SONNET[1] ON CHILLON.

ETERNAL Spirit of the chainless Mind!
Brightest in dungeons, Liberty! thou art,
For there thy habitation is the heart—
The heart which love of thee alone can bind;
And when thy sons to fetters are consigned—   5
To fetters, and the damp vault's dayless gloom,
Their country conquers with their martyrdom,
And Freedom's fame finds wings on every wind.
Chillon! thy prison is a holy place,
And thy sad floor an altar—for 'twas trod,   10
Until his very steps have left a trace
Worn, as if thy cold pavement were a sod,
By Bonnivard![2]   May none those marks efface!
For they appeal from tyranny to God.[3]

[1] The last six lines of this noble introductory sonnet are thrillingly impressive.

[2] François de Bonnivard, a magistrate and political writer of Geneva, suffered six years' imprisonment in Chillon for helping to defend the freedom of Geneva against the duke of Savoy. He was rescued by his countrymen, who captured the castle in the year 1536. This real hero must not be confounded with the imaginary prisoner of the poetical tale. Byron himself wrote: " When this poem was composed I was not sufficiently aware of the history of Bonnivard, or I should have endeavored to dignify the subject by an attempt to celebrate his courage and his virtues."

[3] " His [Byron's] sonnets are all good; the best is that on Bonnivard, one of his noblest and completest poems " (SWINBURNE).

THE PRISONER OF CHILLON.

I.

My hair is gray, but not with years,
    Nor grew it white
    In a single night,
As men's have grown from sudden fears: [1]
My limbs are bowed, though not with toil,   5
    But rusted with a vile repose,
For they have been a dungeon's spoil,
    And mine has been the fate of those
To whom the goodly earth and air
Are banned, and barred—forbidden fare;   10
But this was for my father's faith
I suffered chains and courted death;
That father perished at the stake
For tenets he would not forsake;
And for the same his lineal race   15
In darkness found a dwelling place;
We were seven—who now are one,
    Six in youth, and one in age,
Finished as they had begun,
    Proud of Persecution's rage;   20
One in fire, and two in field,
Their belief with blood have sealed,

[1] Byron cites the case of Ludovico Sforza and of Marie Antoinette.   Are there other instances?

18

Dying as their father died,
For the God their foes denied;
Three were in a dungeon cast,   25
Of whom this wreck is left the last.

II.

There are seven pillars of Gothic mold,
In Chillon's dungeons [1] deep and old,
There are seven columns, massy and gray,
Dim with a dull imprisoned ray,   30
A sunbeam which hath lost its way,
And through the crevice and the cleft
Of the thick wall is fallen and left;
Creeping o'er the floor so damp,
Like a marsh's meteor lamp: [2]   35
And in each pillar there is a ring,
    And in each ring there is a chain;
That iron is a cankering thing,
    For in these limbs its teeth remain,
With marks that will not wear away,   40
Till I have done with this new day,
Which now is painful to these eyes,
Which have not seen the sun so rise
For years—I cannot count them o'er,
I lost their long and heavy score,   45
When my last brother drooped and died,
And I lay living by his side.

[1] The deep old dungeon which suggested the poem is not so gloomy as the verses would indicate.   Longfellow called it a "'delightful dungeon."   " In the cells," wrote Byron, " are seven pillars, or rather eight, one being half merged in the wall.   In some of these are rings for the fetters and the fettered. On the pavement the steps of Bonnivard have left their traces."

[2] A meteor is any atmospheric phenomenon.   Marsh gas takes fire spontaneously on coming in contact with oxygen.   Byron's " meteor lamp " is the

III.

They chained us each to a column stone,[1]
And we were three—yet, each alone;
We could not move a single pace,   50
We could not see each other's face,
But with that pale and livid light
That made us strangers in our sight:
And thus together—yet apart,
Fettered in hand, but joined in heart,   55
'Twas still some solace, in the dearth
Of the pure elements of earth,
To hearken to each other's speech,
And each turn comforter to each
With some new hope, or legend old,   60
Or song heroically bold;
But even these at length grew cold.
Our voices took a dreary tone,
An echo of the dungeon stone,
   A grating sound, not full and free,   65
   As they of yore were wont to be:
   It might be fancy, but to me
They never sounded like our own.

IV.

I was the eldest of the three,
   And to uphold and cheer the rest   70
   I ought to do—and did my best—
And each did well in his degree.

ignis fatuus or will-o'-the-wisp, the Jack-o'-lantern of superstition. (See Milton's L'Allegro for " friar's lantern.")

[1] Byron's name, graved by his own hand, is on the central " column stone," the one to which Bonnivard was chained.

The youngest, whom my father loved,
Because our mother's brow was given
To him, with eyes as blue as heaven—   75
    For him my soul was sorely moved;
And truly might it be distressed
To see such bird in such a nest;
For he was beautiful as day—
    (When day was beautiful to me   80
    As to young eagles, being [1] free)—
    A polar day,[2] which will not see
A sunset till its summer's gone,
    Its sleepless summer of long light,
The snow-clad offspring of the sun: 85
    And thus he was as pure and bright,
And in his natural spirit gay,
With tears for naught but others' ills,
And then they flowed like mountain rills,
Unless he could assuage the woe   90
Which he abhorred to view below.[3]

V.

The other was as pure of mind,
But formed to combat with his kind;
Strong in his frame, and of a mood
Which 'gainst the world in war had stood,   95
And perished in the foremost rank
    With joy:—but not in chains to pine:
His spirit withered with their clank,
    I saw it silently decline—
    And so perchance in sooth did mine: 100

[1] What does "being" modify, "me" or "eagles"?
[2] Why not a *tropical* day?
[3] What part of speech is "below"?   Is the line good?

But yet I forced it on to cheer
Those relics of a home so dear.
He was a hunter of the hills,
  Had followed there the deer and wolf;
  To him his dungeon was a gulf,   105
And fettered feet the worst of ills.

VI.

  Lake Leman [1] lies by Chillon's walls: [2]
A thousand feet in depth below
Its massy waters meet and flow;
Thus much the fathom line was sent   110
From Chillon's snow-white battlement,
  Which round about the wave inthralls:
A double dungeon wall and wave
Have made—and like a living grave
Below the surface of the lake   115
The dark vault lies wherein we lay, [3]
We heard it ripple night and day;
  Sounding o'er our heads it knocked;
And I have felt the winter's spray
Wash through the bars when winds were high   120
And wanton in the happy sky;
  And then the very rock hath rocked,
  And I have felt it shake, unshocked,
Because I could have smiled to see
The death that would have set me free.   125

[1] Leman, ancient classic name for Lake Geneva. (See Childe Harold, Canto III. Stanza LXXXV.: " Clear, placid Leman!" etc.)

[2] " The lake has been fathomed to the depth of eight hundred feet, French measure. . . . The walls are white" (BYRON). The castle with its loopholed towers, once a ducal residence, was used as both fortress and state prison. Parts of the structure are said to be nearly one thousand years old. It is on an isolated rock at the east end of Lake Geneva.

[3] The dungeon is not below the surface of the lake.

VII.

I said my nearer [1] brother pined,
I said his mighty heart declined,
He loathed and put away his food;
It was not that 'twas coarse and rude,
For we were used to hunter's fare,   130
And for the like had little care;
The milk drawn from the mountain goat
Was changed for water from the moat,
Our bread was such as captives' tears
Have moistened many a thousand years,   135
Since man first pent his fellow-men
Like brutes within an iron den;
But what were these to us or him?
These wasted not his heart or limb;
My brother's soul was of that mold   140
Which in a palace had grown cold,
Had his free breathing been denied
The range of the steep mountain's side;
But why delay the truth?—he died.
I saw, and could not hold his head,   145
Nor reach his dying hand—nor dead,—
Though hard I strove, but strove in vain,
To rend and gnash my bonds in twain.
He died, and they unlocked his chain,
And scooped for him a shallow grave   150
Even from the cold earth of our cave.
I begged them as a boon to lay
His corse in dust whereon the day
Might shine—it was a foolish thought,
But then within my brain it wrought,   155
That even in death his freeborn breast
In such a dungeon could not rest.

[1] Nearer in what, distance or age?

I might have spared my idle prayer—
They coldly laughed, and laid him there:
The flat and turfless earth above   160
The being we so much did love;
His empty[1] chain above it leant,[1]
Such murder's fitting monument!

VIII.

But he, the favorite and the flower,
Most cherished since his natal hour,   165
His mother's image in fair face,
The infant love of all his race,
His martyred father's dearest thought,
My latest care, for whom I sought
To hoard my life, that his might be   170
Less wretched now, and one day free;
He, too, who yet had held untired
A spirit natural or inspired[2]—
He, too, was struck, and day by day
Was withered on the stalk away.[3]   175
Oh, God! it is a fearful thing
To see the human soul take wing
In any shape, in any mood:
I've seen it rushing forth in blood,
I've seen it on the breaking ocean   180
Strive with a swoln convulsive motion,
I've seen the sick and ghastly bed
Of Sin delirious with its dread;
But these were horrors—this was woe
Unmixed with such[4]—but sure and slow: 185

[1] Note the inaccuracy of the words "empty" and "leant." Bonnivard's chain, about four feet in length, is preserved among the prison relics.
[2] Inspired by what?
[3] Why "*on* the stalk" rather than "*off* the stalk"?
[4] What does "such" modify? Compare this description with Halleck's

He faded, and so calm and meek,
So softly worn, so sweetly weak,
So tearless, yet so tender, kind,
And grieved for those he left behind;
With all the while a cheek whose bloom   190
Was as a mockery of the tomb,[1]
Whose tints as gently sunk away
As a departing rainbow's ray;
An eye of most transparent light,
That almost made the dungeon bright,   195
And not a word of murmur, not
A groan o'er his untimely lot,—
A little talk of better days,
A little hope my own to raise,
For I was sunk in silence—lost   200
In this last loss, of all the most;
And then the sighs he would suppress
Of fainting nature's feebleness,
More slowly drawn, grew less and less:
I listened, but I could not hear;   205
I called, for I was wild with fear;
I knew 'twas hopeless, but my dread
Would not be thus admonishèd;
I called, and thought I heard a sound[2]—
I burst my chain with one strong bound,   210
And rushed to him:—I found him not,
I only stirred in this black spot,
I only lived, *I* only drew
The accursèd breath of dungeon dew;[3]
The last, the sole, the dearest link   215
Between me and the eternal brink,

lines on modes of death in the poem " Marco Bozzaris : " " Come to the bridal chamber, Death!" etc.
[1] Comment on this line.   [2] Scan this line.
[3] What is "dungeon dew"?

Which bound me to my failing race,
Was broken in this fatal place.
One on the earth, and one beneath [1]—
My brothers—both had ceased to breathe: 220
I took that hand which lay so still,
Alas! my own was full as chill;
I had not strength to stir, or strive,
But felt that I was still alive—
A frantic feeling, when we know   225
That what we love shall ne'er be so.
    I know not why
    I could not die,
I had no earthly hope but faith,
And that forbade a selfish death.   230

IX.

What next befell me then and there
    I know not well—I never knew—
First came the loss of light, and air,
    And then of darkness too:
I had no thought, no feeling—none—   235
Among the stones I stood a stone,
And was, scarce conscious what I wist,
As shrubless crags within the mist; [2]
For all was blank, and bleak, and gray;
It was not night, it was not day;   240
It was not even the dungeon light,
So hateful to my heavy sight,
But vacancy absorbing space, [3]
And fixedness without a place;

---

[1] Study carefully lines 216–219. Are they clear? What is " the eternal brink "?

[2] Can you conceive this image?

[3] Try to imagine " vacancy absorbing space."

There were no stars, no earth, no time,   245
No check, no change, no good, no crime,
But silence, and a stirless breath
Which neither was of life nor death;
A sea of stagnant idleness,
Blind, boundless, mute, and motionless!   250

                    X.

A light broke in upon my brain,—
    It was the carol of a bird;
It ceased, and then it came again,
    The sweetest song ear ever heard,
And mine was thankful till my eyes   255
Ran over with the glad surprise,
And they that moment could not see
I was the mate of misery;
But then by dull degrees came back
My senses to their wonted track;   260
I saw the dungeon walls and floor
Close slowly round me as before,
I saw the glimmer of the sun
Creeping as it before had done,
But through the crevice where it came   265
That bird was perched,[1] as fond and tame,
    And tamer than upon the tree;
A lovely bird, with azure wings,
And song that said a thousand things,
    And seemed to say them all for me!   270
I never saw its like before,
I ne'er shall see its likeness more:
It seemed like me to want a mate,
But was not half so desolate,

---

[1] How could the bird be perched through a crevice?

And it was come to love me when   275
None lived to love me so again,
And cheering from my dungeon's brink,
Had brought me back to feel and think.
I know not if it late were free,
    Or broke its cage to perch on mine,   280
But knowing well captivity,
    Sweet bird! I could not wish for thine!
Or if it were, in wingèd guise,
A visitant from Paradise;
For—Heaven forgive that thought! the while   285
Which made me both to weep and smile—
I sometimes deemed that it might be
My brother's soul come down to me;
But then at last away it flew,
And then 'twas mortal well I knew,   290
For he would never thus have flown,
And left me twice so doubly lone,
Lone as the corse within its shroud,
Lone as a solitary cloud,—
    A single cloud on a sunny day,   295
While all the rest of heaven is clear,
A frown upon the atmosphere,
That hath no business to appear
    When skies are blue, and earth is gay.

XI.

A kind of change came in my fate,   300
My keepers grew compassionate;
I know not what had made them so,[1]
They were inured to sights of woe,
But so it was:—my broken chain
With links unfastened did remain,   305

[1] Does the reader know what had made them so?

And it was liberty to stride
Along my cell from side to side,
And up and down, and then athwart,
And tread it over every part;
And round the pillars one by one, 310
Returning where my walk begun,
Avoiding only, as I trod,
My brothers' graves without a sod;
For if I thought with heedless tread
My step profaned their lowly bed, 315
My breath came gaspingly and thick,
And my crushed heart fell blind and sick.

XII.

I made a footing in the wall,
    It was not therefrom to escape,
For I had buried one and all 320
    Who loved me in a human shape;
And the whole earth would henceforth be
A wider prison unto me:
No child, no sire, no kin had I,
No partner in my misery; 325
I thought of this, and I was glad,
For thought of them had made me mad;
But I was curious to ascend
To my barred windows, and to bend
Once more, upon the mountains high, 330
The quiet of a loving eye.[1]

XIII.

I saw them, and they were the same,[2]
They were not changed like me in frame;

---

[1] This is much in the spirit of Wordsworth.
[2] Many a tourist climbs to the loopholes of the dungeon, as the prisoner

I saw their thousand years of snow
On high—their wide long lake below,   335
And the blue Rhone in fullest flow;
I heard the torrents leap and gush
O'er channeled rock and broken bush;
I saw the white-walled distant town,
And whiter sails go skimming down;   340
And then there was a little isle,
Which in my very face did smile,
    The only one in view;
A small green isle, it seemed no more,
Scarce broader than my dungeon floor,   345
But in it there were three tall trees,
And o'er it blew the mountain breeze,
And by it there were waters flowing,
And on it there were young flowers growing,
    Of gentle breath and hue.   350
The fish swam by the castle wall,
And they seemed joyous each and all;
The eagle rode the rising blast,
Methought he never flew so fast
As then to me he seemed to fly;   355
And then new tears came in my eye,
And I felt troubled—and would fain
I had not left my recent chain;
And when I did descend again,
The darkness of my dim abode   360
    Fell on me as a heavy load;

did and as Byron did, to view the scene here described. The poet tells us
in prose: "The Château de Chillon is situated between Clarens and Villeneuve.
On its left are the entrances of the Rhone, and opposite are the heights of
Meillerie and the range of Alps above Bôveret and Saint-Gingo. Near it, on
a hill, behind, is a torrent. . . . "Not far from Chillon is a very small island,
the only one I could perceive in my voyage round and over the lake. It contains a few trees (I think not above three), and from its singleness and di-
minutive size has a peculiar effect upon the view."

It was as is a new-dug grave,
Closing o'er one we sought to save,—
And yet my glance, too much oppressed,
Had almost need of such a rest.   365

XIV.

It might be months, or years, or days,
    I kept no count, I took no note,
I had no hope my eyes to raise,
    And clear them of their dreary mote ;
At last men came to set me free ;   370
    I asked not why, and recked not where ;
It was at length the same to me,
Fettered or fetterless to be,
    I learned to love despair.
And thus when they appeared at last,   375
And all my bonds aside were cast,
These heavy walls to me had grown
A hermitage—and all my own !
And half I felt as they were come
To tear me from a second home :   380
With spiders I had friendship made,
And watched them in their sullen trade,
Had seen the mice by moonlight play,
And why should I feel less than they?
We were all inmates of one place,   385
And I, the monarch of each race,
Had power to kill—yet, strange to tell !
In quiet we had learned to dwell ;
My very chains and I grew friends,
So much a long communion tends   390
To make us what we are :—even I
Regained my freedom with a sigh.

QUESTIONS AND SUGGESTIONS FOR
THE STUDENT.

In what historical period are the events of this poem supposed to occur ?   In what lands?

What probably was the religious faith of the prisoners?

Describe the meter of the poem.   Is it suited to such a tale? What other poets used the same metrical form?

Pick out the most poetical passages.

Part IX. is much admired by critics : can you discover its superior merit?

Observe the exquisite tenderness of Part X.

Which lines show Byron's susceptibility to humane emotions? To nature's influence?

Compare, as to body and as to mind, the two brothers who died in prison.

What evidence of their superstitious tendency do the prisoners betray?

It might prove interesting to the reader to compare with this celebrated poem other pieces of literature dealing with the sorrow and heroism of human captivity.   Read Surrey's lines on his imprisonment in Windsor, Sir R. L'Estrange's " Loyalty Confined," and R. Lovelace's " To Althea, from Prison ; " also Scott's description of a dungeon in " Marmion."   In prose, every schoolboy should read " My Prisons," by Silvio Pellico, and " Picciola," by Santaine.

CHILDE HAROLD'S "GOOD NIGHT"[1] TO HIS NATIVE LAND.

1.

ADIEU, adieu! my native shore
Fades o'er the waters blue;
The night winds sigh, the breakers roar,
And shrieks the wild sea mew.
Yon sun that sets upon the sea   5
We follow in his flight;
Farewell awhile to him and thee,
My native Land—Good Night!

2.

A few short hours and he will rise
To give the morrow birth;   10
And I shall hail the main and skies,
But not my mother earth.
Deserted is my own good hall,
Its hearth is desolate;
Wild weeds are gathering on the wall;   15
My dog howls at the gate.

---

[1] This lyric is from the first canto of Childe Harold's Pilgrimage, published in 1812, when the author was but twenty-four. Byron tells us it "was suggested by Lord Maxwell's Good Night, in the Border Minstrelsy, edited by Mr. Scott."

3   33

3.

"Come hither, hither, my little page![1]
    Why dost thou weep and wail?
Or dost thou dread the billows' rage,
    Or tremble at the gale?   20
But dash the tear-drop from thine eye;
    Our ship is swift and strong:
Our fleetest falcon scarce can fly
    More merrily along."

4.

"Let winds be shrill, let waves roll high,   25
    I fear not wave nor wind:
Yet marvel not, Sir Childe, that I
    Am sorrowful in mind;
For I have from my father gone,
    A mother whom I love,   30
And have no friend, save these alone,
    But thee—and one above.

5.

"My father blessed me fervently,
    Yet did not much complain;
But sorely will my mother sigh   35
    Till I come back again."—
"Enough, enough, my little lad!
    Such tears become thine eye;
If I thy guileless bosom had,
    Mine own would not be dry.   40

[1] Robert Rushton, the son of one of Lord Byron's tenants. " I like him,"
wrote Byron to the lad's mother, " because, like myself, he seems a friendless
animal."

6.

" Come hither, hither, my stanch yeoman,[1]
    Why dost thou look so pale?
Or dost thou dread a French foeman? [2]
    Or shiver at the gale? "—
" Deem'st thou I tremble for my life ?   45
    Sir Childe, I'm not so weak;
But thinking on an absent wife
    Will blanch a faithful cheek.

7.

" My spouse and boys dwell near thy hall,
    Along the bordering lake,   50
And when they on their father call,
    What answer shall she make? "—
" Enough, enough, my yeoman good,
    Thy grief let none gainsay;
But I, who am of lighter mood,   55
    Will laugh to flee away."

8.

For who would trust the seeming sighs
    Of wife or paramour?
Fresh feres [3] will dry the bright blue eyes
    We late saw streaming o'er.   60
For pleasures past I do not grieve,
    Nor perils gathering near;
My greatest grief is that I leave
    No thing that claims a tear.[4]

[1] William Fletcher, Byron's faithful valet, who served the poet for twenty
years and was with him when he died at Missolonghi in 1824.
[2] Were the French foemen of the English in 1809?
[3] " Fere," a consort or companion.
[4] Byron wrote to his mother in June, 1809: " The world is all before me,

9.

And now I'm in the world alone,   65
    Upon the wide, wide sea:
But why should I for others groan,
    When none will sigh for me?
Perchance my dog will whine in vain,
    Till fed by stranger hands;   70
But long ere I come back again
    He'd tear me where he stands.

10.

With thee, my bark, I'll swiftly go
    Athwart the foaming brine;
Nor care what land thou bear'st me to,   75
    So not again to mine.
Welcome, welcome, ye dark-blue waves!
    And when you fail my sight,
Welcome, ye deserts and ye caves!
    My native Land—Good Night!   80

and I leave England without regret, and without a wish to revisit anything it contains, except yourself."

CHILDE[1] HAROLD'S PILGRIMAGE.

CANTO THE THIRD.[2]

" Afin que cette application vous forçât de penser à autre chose ; il n'y a en vérité de remède que celui-là et le temps." [3]—*Lettre du Roi de Prusse à D'Alembert, September* 7, 1776.

I.

Is thy face like thy mother's, my fair child!
ADA![4] sole daughter of my house and heart?
When last I saw thy young blue eyes they smiled,
And then we parted,—not as now we part,
But with a hope.—

            Awaking with a start,   5
The waters heave around me ; and on high
The winds lift up their voices : I depart,
Whither I know not ; but the hour's gone by,
When Albion's lessening shores could grieve or glad mine eye.

---

[1] The word " childe," in old poetical usage, means a noble youth, as Childe Waters, Childe Childers. (See Shakespeare's line in Lear, iii. iv., where Edgar sings : " Childe Rowland to the dark tower came.") Byron first called his hero Childe *Burun*, an early form of his own family name.

[2] See Introduction, p. 9, for an account of Cantos I. and II.

[3] Translate this French motto, and explain how it applies to Byron's personal history.

[4] Augusta Ada Byron (born December 10, 1815) was but five weeks old

37

II.

Once more upon the waters![1] yet once more!   10
And the waves bound beneath me as a steed
That knows his rider.   Welcome to their roar!
Swift be their guidance, wheresoe'er it lead!
Though the strained mast should quiver as a reed,
And the rent canvas fluttering strew the gale,   15
Still must I on; for I am as a weed,
Flung from the rock, on Ocean's foam to sail
Where'er the surge may sweep, the tempest's breath prevail.

III.

In my youth's summer I did sing of One,[2]
The wandering outlaw of his own dark mind;   20
Again I seize the theme, then but begun,
And bear it with me, as the rushing wind
Bears the cloud onwards: in that Tale I find
The furrows of long thought, and dried-up tears,
Which, ebbing, leave a sterile track behind,   25
O'er which all heavily the journeying years
Plod the last sands of life,—where not a flower appears.

IV.

Since my young days of passion—joy, or pain,
Perchance my heart and harp have lost a string,

when her father saw her for the last time. On January 5, 1816, he wrote to
the poet Tom Moore: " She was and is very flourishing and fat, and reckoned
very large for her days,—squalls and sucks incessantly." Byron's daughter
married the earl of Lovelace in 1835, and died in 1852.

[1] Byron left England, April 25, 1816, never to return. He made his first
foreign tour in 1809–1810.

[2] Childe Harold.

And both may jar: it may be, that in vain   30
I would essay as I have sung to sing.
Yet, though a dreary strain, to this I cling;
So that it wean me from the weary dream
Of selfish grief or gladness—so it fling
Forgetfulness around me—it shall seem   35
To me, though to none else, a not ungrateful theme.

V.

He who, grown aged in this world of woe,
In deeds, not years,[1] piercing the depths of life,
So that no wonder waits him; nor below
Can love or sorrow, fame, ambition, strife,   40
Cut to his heart again with the keen knife
Of silent, sharp endurance: he can tell
Why thought seeks refuge in lone caves, yet rife
With airy images, and shapes which dwell
Still unimpaired, though old, in the soul's haunted cell.   45

VI.

'Tis to create, and in creating live
A being more intense, that we endow
With form our fancy, gaining as we give
The life we image, even as I do now.[2]
What am I?   Nothing: but not so art thou,   50
Soul of my thought! with whom I traverse earth,
Invisible but gazing, as I glow
Mixed with thy spirit, blended with thy birth,
And feeling still with thee in my crushed feelings' dearth.

[1] " We live in deeds, not years " (BAILEY's Festus).
[2] The poet finds refuge from the troubles of life in the exercise of literary imagination. Longfellow sings of " the rapture of creating."   Byron's ideal, the " soul of his thought," was superior to his actual self.

VII.

Yet must I think less wildly : — I *have* thought   55
Too long and darkly, till my brain became,
In its own eddy boiling and o'erwrought,
A whirling gulf of fantasy and flame :
And thus, untaught in youth my heart to tame,
My springs of life were poisoned.[1]   'Tis too late!   60
Yet am I changed; though still enough the same
In strength to bear what time cannot abate,
And feed on bitter fruits without accusing Fate.

VIII.

Something too much of this :[2]—but now 'tis past,
And the spell closes with its silent seal.   65
Long-absent HAROLD reappears at last;
He of the breast which fain no more would feel,
Wrung with the wounds which kill not, but ne'er heal;
Yet Time, who changes all, had altered him
In soul and aspect as in age: years steal   70
Fire from the mind as vigor from the limb;
And life's enchanted cup but sparkles near the brim.

IX.

His had been quaffed too quickly, and he found
The dregs were wormwood; but he filled again,
And from a purer fount,[3] on holier ground,[3]   75
And deemed its spring perpetual; but in vain!

[1] This refers bitterly to the author's neglected childhood. He blames circumstances.   [2] See Hamlet, iii. ii.

[3] What "fount" on what "holier ground"? Seek the answer in the stanzas following. The first sixteen stanzas are introductory and largely egotistical.

Still round him clung invisibly a chain
Which galled forever, fettering though unseen,
And heavy, though it clanked not; worn with pain,
Which pined although it spoke not, and grew keen,   80
Entering with every step he took through many a scene.

X.

Secure in guarded coldness, he had mixed
Again in fancied safety with his kind,
And deemed his spirit now so firmly fixed
And sheathed with an invulnerable mind,   85
That, if no joy, no sorrow lurked behind;
And he, as one, might 'midst the many stand
Unheeded, searching through the crowd to find
Fit speculation; such as in strange land
He found in wonder works of God and Nature's hand.   90

XI.

But who can view the ripened rose, nor seek
To wear it? who can curiously behold
The smoothness and the sheen[1] of beauty's cheek,
Nor feel the heart can never all[2] grow old?
Who can contemplate Fame through clouds unfold   95
The star which rises o'er her steep, nor climb?
Harold, once more within the vortex, rolled
On with the giddy circle, chasing Time,
Yet with a nobler aim than in his youth's fond[3] prime.

XII.

But soon he knew himself the most unfit   100
Of men to herd with Man; with whom he held

---

[1] Look up the word " sheen " in your dictionary.   " The sheen on their spears was like stars on the sea " (BYRON).
[2] Altogether.   [3] Foolish.

Little in common; untaught to submit
His thoughts to others, though his soul was quelled
In youth by his own thoughts; still uncompelled,
He would not yield dominion of his mind   105
To spirits against whom his own rebelled;
Proud though in desolation; which could find
A life within itself, to breathe without mankind.

XIII.

Where rose the mountains, there to him were friends;
Where rolled the ocean, thereon was his home;   110
Where a blue sky, and glowing clime, extends,
He had the passion and the power to roam;
The desert, forest, cavern, breaker's foam,
Were unto him companionship; they spake
A mutual language, clearer than the tome   115
Of his land's tongue, which he would oft forsake
For Nature's pages glassed by sunbeams on the lake

XIV.

Like the Chaldean, he could watch the stars,
Till he had peopled them with beings bright
As their own beams; and earth, and earth-born jars,   120
And human frailties, were forgotten quite:
Could he have kept his spirit to that flight,
He had been happy; but this clay will sink
Its spark immortal, envying it the light
To which it mounts, as if to break the link   125
That keeps us from yon heaven which wooes us to its brink.[1]

XV.

But in Man's dwellings he became a thing
Restless and worn, and stern and wearisome,

[1] See Prisoner of Chillon, line 216.

Drooped as a wild-born falcon with clipped wing,
To whom the boundless air alone were home: 130
Then came his fit again,[1] which to o'ercome,
As eagerly the barred-up bird will beat
His breast and beak against his wiry dome
Till the blood tinge his plumage, so the heat
Of his impeded soul would through his bosom eat.   135

XVI.

Self-exiled Harold wanders forth again,
With naught of hope left, but with less of gloom;
The very knowledge that he lived in vain,
That all was over on this side the tomb,
Had made Despair a smilingness assume,   140
Which, though 'twere wild,—as on the plundered wreck
When mariners would madly meet their doom   ·
With draughts intemperate on the sinking deck,—
Did yet inspire a cheer, which he forbore to check.[2]

XVII.

Stop![3]—for thy tread is on an Empire's dust!   145
An Earthquake's spoil is sepulchered below!
Is the spot marked with no colossal bust?[4]
Nor column trophied for triumphal show?

[1] See Macbeth, iii. iv.

[2] "In the first sixteen stanzas there is a mighty but groaning burst of dark and appalling strength" (Sir EGERTON BRYDGES). "These stanzas —in which the author, adopting more distinctly the character of Childe Harold than in the original poem, assigns the cause why he has resumed his pilgrim's staff when it was hoped he had sat down for life, a denizen of his native country—abound with much moral interest and poetical beauty." Let the pupil point out passages characterized by moral interest or poetical beauty.

[3] Mark the abrupt transition,—like a sudden drumbeat. The next twelve powerful stanzas show Byron's genius at its best.

[4] A monument now marks the field of Waterloo.

None; but the moral's truth tells simpler so,
As the ground was before, thus let it be;—   150
How that red rain hath made the harvest grow!
And is this all the world has gained by thee,
Thou first and last of fields! king-making Victory?

XVIII.

And Harold stands upon this place of skulls,[1]
The grave of France, the deadly Waterloo!   155
How in an hour the power which gave annuls
Its gifts, transferring fame as fleeting too!
In "pride of place"[2] here last the eagle flew,
Then tore with bloody talon the rent plain,
Pierced by the shaft of banded nations through;   160
Ambition's life and labors all were vain;
He wears the shattered links of the world's broken chain.

XIX.[3]

Fit retribution! Gaul may champ the bit
And foam in fetters;—but is Earth more free?
Did nations combat to make *One* submit;   165
Or league to teach all kings true sovereignty?
What! shall reviving Thraldom again be
The patched-up idol of enlightened days?[4]
Shall we, who struck the Lion down, shall we
Pay the Wolf homage? proffering lowly gaze   170
And servile knees to thrones? No; *prove* before ye praise!

---

[1] Byron visited the field of Waterloo a year after the battle had been fought.

[2] "'Pride of place' is a term of falconry and means the highest pitch of flight" (BYRON).

[3] Determine the metaphorical force of "Gaul," "Earth," "One," "Thraldom," "Lion," and "Wolf" in this stanza.

[4] "Upon the downfall of Napoleon, Alexander I. of Russia organized the

XX.

If not, o'er one fallen despot boast no more!
In vain fair cheeks were furrowed with hot tears
For Europe's flowers long rooted up before
The trampler of her vineyards; in vain years   175
Of death, depopulation, bondage, fears,
Have all been borne, and broken by the accord
Of roused-up millions: all that most endears
Glory, is when the myrtle wreathes a sword
Such as Harmodius drew on Athens' tyrant lord.[1]   180

XXI.

There was a sound of revelry by night,[2]
And Belgium's capital had gathered then
Her Beauty and her Chivalry, and bright
The lamps shone o'er fair women and brave men;
A thousand hearts beat happily; and when   185
Music arose with its voluptuous swell,
Soft eyes looked love to eyes which spake again,
And all went merry as a marriage bell;
But hush! hark! a deep sound strikes like a rising knell!

XXII.

Did ye not hear it?—No; 'twas but the wind,   190
Or the car rattling o'er the stony street;

Holy Alliance, a league embracing Russia, Austria, and Prussia. But the
Holy Alliance very soon became practically a league for the maintenance of
absolute principles of government in opposition to the liberal tendencies of
the age " (Dr. P. V. N. MYERS).

1 " When Hippias and Hipparchus, sons of Pisistratus, were tyrants of
Athens, two friends, Harmodius and Aristogiton, conspired against them, and
killed Hipparchus with daggers concealed in the myrtle branches which they
carried " (H. F. TOZER's Childe Harold).

2 There was a ball at Brussels on the night of June 15, 1815. The battle

On with the dance! let joy be unconfined;
No sleep till morn, when Youth and Pleasure meet
To chase the glowing Hours with flying feet—
But hark!—that heavy sound breaks in once more,   195
As if the clouds its echo would repeat;
And nearer, clearer, deadlier than before!
Arm! Arm! it is—it is—the cannon's opening roar!

XXIII.

Within a windowed niche of that high hall
Sate Brunswick's fated chieftain;[1] he did hear   200
That sound the first amidst the festival,
And caught its tone with Death's prophetic ear;
And when they smiled because he deemed it near,
His heart more truly knew that peal too well
Which stretched his father on a bloody bier,   205
And roused the vengeance blood alone could quell;
He rushed into the field, and, foremost fighting, fell.

XXIV.

Ah! then and there was hurrying to and fro,
And gathering tears, and tremblings of distress,
And cheeks all pale, which but an hour ago   210
Blushed at the praise of their own loveliness;
And there were sudden partings, such as press
The life from out young hearts, and choking sighs
Which ne'er might be repeated: who could guess
If ever more should meet those mutual eyes,   215
Since upon night so sweet such awful morn could rise!

of Quatre Bras was fought June 16, and that of Waterloo proper on the 18th.
Read some good history of these great events.

[1] The duke of Brunswick fell at Quatre Bras; his father was killed at Jena
in 1806.

XXV.

And there was mounting in hot haste : the steed,
The mustering squadron, and the clattering car,
Went pouring forward with impetuous speed,
And swiftly forming in the ranks of war;   220
And the deep thunder peal on peal afar;
And near, the beat of the alarming drum
Roused up the soldier ere the morning star;
While thronged the citizens with terror dumb,
Or whispering, with white lips—"The foe!   They come!
   they come!"   225

XXVI.

And wild and high the "Cameron's gathering"[1] rose!
The war note of Lochiel,[2] which Albyn's[3] hills
Have heard, and heard, too, have her Saxon foes:—
How in the noon of night that pibroch[4] thrills,
Savage and shrill!   But with the breath which fills   230
Their mountain pipe, so fill the mountaineers
With the fierce native daring which instills
The stirring memory of a thousand years,
And Evan's, Donald's fame rings in each clansman's ears![5]

XXVII.

And Ardennes[6] waves above them her green leaves,   235
Dewy with Nature's tear-drops, as they pass,

[1] A Scottish clan.
[2] Lochiel, chief of the clan.   (See Lochiel's Warning, by Campbell.)
[3] The old Gaelic name of Scotland.
[4] Martial music of the bagpipe.
[5] " Sir Evan Cameron, and his descendant Donald, the ' gentle Lochiel '
the ' forty-five ' " (BYRON).
[6] The wood of Soignies, not far from the Belgian forest of Ardennes, but

Grieving, if aught inanimate e'er grieves,
Over the unreturning brave,—alas!
Ere evening to be trodden like the grass
Which now beneath them, but above shall grow   240
In its next verdure, when this fiery mass
Of living valor, rolling on the foe
And burning with high hope, shall molder cold and low.

XXVIII.

Last noon beheld them full of lusty life,
Last eve in Beauty's circle proudly gay,   245
The midnight brought the signal sound of strife,
The morn the marshaling in arms,—the day
Battle's magnificently stern array!
The thunderclouds close o'er it, which when rent
The earth is covered thick with other clay,   250
Which her own clay shall cover, heaped and pent,
Rider and horse,—friend, foe,—in one red burial blent!

XXIX.

Their praise is hymned by loftier harps than mine: [1]
Yet one I would select from that proud throng,
Partly because they blend me with his line,   255
And partly that I did his sire [2] some wrong,
And partly that bright names will hallow song; [3]
And his was of the bravest, and when showered

---

not, as Byron supposed, identical with the Arden of Shakespeare's As You Like It, which is in England.

[1] In compliment to Scott and others.

[2] The "sire" was Lord Carlisle, Byron's guardian, whose writing is called, in English Bards and Scotch Reviewers, "the paralytic puling of Carlisle."

[3] This is the first double dissyllabic rime in the poem.

The death bolts deadliest the thinned files along,
Even where the thickest of war's tempest lowered,   260
They reached no nobler breast than thine, young, gallant
    Howard![1]

XXX.

There have been tears and breaking hearts for thee,
And mine were nothing, had I such to give ;
But when I stood beneath the fresh green tree,
Which living waves where thou didst cease to live,   265
And saw around me the wide field revive
With fruits and fertile promise, and the Spring
Come forth her work of gladness to contrive,
With all her reckless birds upon the wing,
I turned from all she brought to those she could not bring.[2] 270

XXXI.

I turned to thee, to thousands, of whom each
And one as all a ghastly gap did make
In his own kind and kindred, whom to teach
Forgetfulness were mercy for their sake ;
The Archangel's trump, not Glory's, must awake   275
Those whom they thirst for ; though the sound of Fame
May for a moment soothe, it cannot slake
The fever of vain longing, and the name
So honored but assumes a stronger, bitterer claim.

XXXII.

They mourn, but smile at length ; and, smiling,   280
The tree will wither long before it fall ;
The hull drives on, though mast and sail be torn ;

[1] Major Frederick Howard, whose grave Byron visited.
[2] Professor E. H. Keene calls attention to the " exquisite couplet which concludes this stanza." Find the most felicitous touch in the two lines.

4

The rooftree sinks, but molders on the hall
In massy hoariness; the ruined wall
Stands when its wind-worn battlements are gone;   285
The bars survive the captive they enthrall;
The day drags through, though storms keep out the sun;
And thus the heart will break, yet brokenly live on: [1]

XXXIII.

Even as a broken mirror, which the glass
In every fragment multiplies; and makes   290
A thousand images of one that was,
The same, and still the more, the more it breaks;
And thus the heart will do which not forsakes,
Living in shattered guise; and still, and cold,
And bloodless, with its sleepless sorrow aches,   295
Yet withers on till all without is old,
Showing no visible sign, for such things are untold.[2]

XXXIV.

There is a very life in our despair,
Vitality of poison,—a quick root
Which feeds these deadly branches; for it were   300
As nothing did we die; but Life will suit
Itself to Sorrow's most detested fruit,
Like to the apples on the Dead Sea's shore,[3]
All ashes to the taste: Did man compute
Existence by enjoyment, and count o'er   305
Such hours 'gainst years of life,—say, would he name three-
         score?

[1] Observe the metaphors in Stanza XXXII., and how they describe lingering grief.

[2] The simile of the broken mirror has been much admired and praised. Read it attentively.

[3] " The (fabled) apples on the brink of the lake Asphaltes were said to be fair without, and within ashes " (BYRON).

XXXV.

The Psalmist numbered out the years of man : [1]
They are enough ; and if thy tale [2] be *true*,
Thou, who didst grudge him even that fleeting span,
More than enough, thou fatal Waterloo!   310
Millions of tongues record thee, and anew
Their children's lips shall echo them, and say—
" Here, where the sword united nations drew,
Our countrymen were warring on that day!"
And this is much, and all which will not pass away.   315

XXXVI.

There sunk the greatest, nor the worst of men,[3]
Whose spirit, antithetically mixed,
One moment of the mightiest, and again
On little objects with like firmness fixed ;
Extreme in all things! hadst thou been betwixt,   320
Thy throne had still been thine, or never been ;
For daring made thy rise as fall : thou seek'st
Even now to reassume the imperial mien,
And shake again the world, the Thunderer of the scene!

XXXVII.

Conqueror and captive of the earth art thou!   325
She trembles at thee still, and thy wild name
Was ne'er more bruited [4] in men's minds than now
That thou art nothing, save the jest of Fame,
Who wooed thee once, thy vassal, and became
The flatterer of thy fierceness, till thou wert   330

---

1 " The days of our years are threescore years and ten " (Ps. xc. 10).
2 " Tale " means what?
3 Stanzas XXXVI.-XLI. give Byron's ideas of Napoleon.
4 Reported. " Thou art no less than fame hath bruited " (I. Henry VI.,
ii. i.).

A god unto thyself; nor less the same
To the astounded kingdoms all inert,
Who deemed thee for a time whate'er thou didst assert.

XXXVIII.

Oh, more or less than man—in high or low,
Battling with nations, flying from the field;   335
Now making monarchs' necks thy footstool, now
More than thy meanest soldier taught to yield;
An empire thou couldst crush, command, rebuild,
But govern not thy pettiest passion, nor,
However deeply in men's spirits skilled,   340
Look through thine own, nor curb the lust of war,
Nor learn that tempted Fate will leave the loftiest star.

XXXIX.

Yet well thy soul hath brooked the turning tide
With that untaught innate philosophy,
Which, be it wisdom, coldness, or deep pride,   345
Is gall and wormwood to an enemy.
When the whole host of hatred stood hard by,
To watch and mock thee shrinking, thou hast smiled
With a sedate and all-enduring eye;—
When Fortune fled her spoiled and favorite child,   350
He stood unbowed beneath the ills upon him piled.[1]

XL.

Sager than in thy fortunes; for in them
Ambition steeled thee on too far to show
That just habitual scorn, which could contemn
Men and their thoughts; 'twas wise to feel, not so   355

[1] Byron admired fortitude.

To wear it ever on thy lip and brow,
And spurn the instruments thou wert to use
Till they were turned unto thine overthrow:
'Tis but a worthless world to win or lose;
So hath it proved to thee, and all such lot who choose.   360

XLI.

If, like a tower upon a headland rock,[1]
Thou hadst been made to stand or fall alone,
Such scorn of man had helped to brave the shock;
But men's thoughts were the steps which paved thy throne,
Their admiration thy best weapon shone;   365
The part of Philip's son was thine, not then
(Unless aside thy purple had been thrown)
Like stern Diogenes to mock at men;
For sceptered cynics earth were far too wide a den.[2]

XLII.[3]

But quiet to quick bosoms is a hell,   370
And *there* hath been thy bane; there is a fire
And motion of the soul which will not dwell
In its own narrow being, but aspire
Beyond the fitting medium of desire;
And, but once kindled, quenchless evermore,   375
Preys upon high adventure, nor can tire
Of aught but rest; a fever at the core,
Fatal to him who bears, to all who ever bore.

---

[1] Steep.

[2] "The great error of Napoleon," says Byron, "was a continued obtrusion mankind of his want of all community of feeling for or with them." ogenes, in his tub, may mock at men, but Alexander, if he wishes to rule : world, cannot afford to be a cynic.

[3] This and the two following stanzas form an interesting poetical study of ibition, a passion to which Byron himself was not a stranger. The lines : strong and suggestive.

XLIII.

This makes the madmen who have made men mad
By their contagion: Conquerors and Kings,   380
Founders of sects and systems, to whom add
Sophists, Bards, Statesmen, all unquiet things
Which stir too strongly the soul's secret springs,
And are themselves the fools to those they fool;
Envied, yet how unenviable! what stings   385
Are theirs!   One breast laid open were a school
Which would unteach mankind the lust to shine or rule:

XLIV.

Their breath is agitation, and their life
A storm whereon they ride, to sink at last,
And yet so nursed and bigoted to strife,   390
That should their days, surviving perils past,
Melt to calm twilight, they feel overcast
With sorrow and supineness, and so die;
Even as a flame unfed, which runs to waste
With its own flickering, or a sword laid by,   395
Which eats into itself, and rusts ingloriously.

XLV.[1]

He who ascends to mountain tops, shall find
The loftiest peaks most wrapt in clouds and snow;
He who surpasses or subdues mankind,
Must look down on the hate of those below.   400
Though high *above* the sun of glory glow,
And far *beneath* the earth and ocean spread,
Round him are icy rocks, and loudly blow
Contending tempests on his naked head,
And thus reward the toils which to those summits led. 405

[1] Point out the fallacy in this stanza.

XLVI.

Away with these! true Wisdom's world will be
Within its own creation, or in thine,
Maternal Nature![1] for who teems like thee,
Thus on the banks of thy majestic Rhine?[2]
There Harold gazes on a work divine,   410
A blending of all beauties; streams and dells,
Fruit, foliage, crag, wood, cornfield, mountain, vine,
And chiefless castles breathing stern farewells
From gray but leafy walls, where Ruin greenly dwells.[3]

XLVII.

And there they stand, as stands a lofty mind,   415
Worn, but unstooping to the baser crowd,
All tenantless, save to the crannying wind,[4]
Or holding dark communion with the crowd.
There was a day when they were young and proud;
Banners on high, and battles passed below;   420
But they who fought are in a bloody shroud,
And those which waved are shredless dust ere now,
And the bleak battlements shall bear no future blow.

XLVIII.

Beneath these battlements, within those walls,
Power dwelt amidst her passions; in proud state   425
Each robber chief upheld his armèd halls,
Doing his evil will, nor less elate

[1] "The transition from the subject of Napoleon to that of the Rhine is made by contrasting ambition with the love of nature " (Tozer).

[2] What literature pertaining to the Rhine have you read?

[3] Observe the force and beauty of the last four lines.

[4] Blowing through crannies. Recall Tennyson's Flower in the Crannied Wall.

Than mightier heroes of a longer date.
What want these outlaws conquerors should have [1]
But History's purchased page to call them great?   430
A wider space, an ornamented grave?
Their hopes were not less warm, their souls were full as brave.

XLIX.

In their baronial feuds and single fields,
What deeds of prowess unrecorded died!
And Love, which lent a blazon to their shields,   435
With emblems well devised by amorous pride,
Through all the mail of iron hearts would glide;
But still their flame was fierceness, and drew on
Keen contest and destruction near allied,
And many a tower for some fair mischief won,   440
Saw the discolored Rhine beneath its ruin run.

L.

But Thou, exulting and abounding river!
Making thy waves a blessing as they flow
Through banks whose beauty would endure forever,
Could man but leave thy bright creation so,   445
Nor its fair promise from the surface mow
With the sharp scythe of conflict,—then to see
.Thy valley of sweet waters, were to know
Earth paved like Heaven; and to seem such to me,   449
Even now what wants thy stream?—that it should Lethe be.[2]

---

[1] "'What wants that knave that a king should have?' was King James's
question on meeting Johnny Armstrong and his followers in full accouter-
ments" (BYRON).

[2] The Rhine would seem heavenly if, like Lethe, it could cause forgetfulness of the past.

LI.[1]

A thousand battles have assailed thy banks,
But these and half their fame have passed away,
And Slaught heaped on high his weltering ranks;
Their very graves are gone, and what are they?
Thy tide washed down the blood of yesterday,　　　455
And all was stainless, and on thy clear stream
Glassed, with its dancing light, the sunny ray;
But o'er the blackened memory's blighting dream
Thy waves would vainly roll, all sweeping as they seem.

LII.

Thus Harold inly said, and passed along,　　　460
Yet not insensible to all which here
Awoke the jocund birds to early song
In glens which might have made even exile dear:
Though on his brow were graven lines austere,
And tranquil sternness, which had ta'en the place　　　465
Of feelings fierier far but less severe,
Joy was not always absent from his face,
But o'er it in such scenes would steal with transient trace.

LIII.

Nor was all love shut from him, though his days
Of passion had consumed themselves to dust.　　　470
It is in vain that we would coldly gaze
On such as smile upon us; the heart must
Leap kindly back to kindness, though disgust
Hath weaned it from all worldlings: thus he felt,

---

[1] A fine stanza, musical and impressive.

For there was soft remembrance and sweet trust   475
In one fond breast,[1] to which his own would melt,
And in its tenderer hour on that his bosom dwelt.

LIV.

And he had learned to love,—I know not why,
For this in such as him seems strange of mood,—
The helpless looks of blooming infancy,   480
Even in its earliest nurture; what subdued,
To change like this, a mind so far imbued
With scorn of man, it little boots to know;
But thus it was; and though in solitude
Small power the nipped affections have to grow,   485
In him this glowed when all beside had ceased to glow.

LV.

And there was one soft breast, as hath been said,
Which unto his was bound by stronger ties
Than the church links withal; and, though unwed,
That love was pure, and, far above disguise,   490
Had stood the test of mortal enmities
Still undivided, and cemented more
By peril, dreaded most in female eyes;
But this was firm, and from a foreign shore
Well to that heart might his these absent greetings pour!   495

I.

The castled crag of Drachenfels[2]
Frowns o'er the wide and winding Rhine,

[1] This refers to Byron's half-sister Augusta, to whom the lyric that follows was written in May, 1816.

[2] "The castle of Drachenfels stands on the highest summit of the 'Seven Mountains,' over the Rhine banks. It is in ruins, and connected with some singular traditions. It is the first in view on the road from Bonn, but on the

Whose breast of waters broadly swells
Between the banks which bear the vine,
And hills all rich with blossomed trees,   500
And fields which promise corn and wine,
And scattered cities crowning these,
Whose far white walls along them shine,
Have strewed a scene, which I should see
With double joy wert *thou* with me.   505

2.

And peasant girls, with deep-blue eyes,
And hands which offer early flowers,
Walk smiling o'er this paradise;
Above, the frequent feudal towers
Through green leaves lift their walls of gray;   510
And many a rock which steeply lowers,
And noble arch in proud decay,
Look o'er this vale of vintage bowers;
But one thing want these banks of Rhine,—
Thy gentle hand to clasp in mine!   515

3.

I send the lilies given to me;
Though long before thy hand they touch,
I know that they must withered be,
But yet reject them not as such;
For I have cherished them as dear,   520
Because they yet may meet thine eye,
And guide thy soul to mine even here,
When thou behold'st them drooping nigh,
And know'st them gathered by the Rhine,
And offered from my heart to thine!   525

opposite side of the river" (BYRON). The word "Drachenfels" means
"Dragon's Rock."

4.

The river nobly foams and flows,
The charm of this enchanted ground,
And all its thousand turns disclose
Some fresher beauty varying round :
The haughtiest breast its wish might bound   530
Through life to dwell delighted here ;
Nor could on earth a spot be found
To Nature and to me so dear,
Could thy dear eyes in following mine
Still sweeten more these banks of Rhine!   535

LVI.

By Coblenz,[1] on a rise of gentle ground,
There is a small and simple pyramid,
Crowning the summit of the verdant mound ;
Beneath its base are heroes' ashes hid,
Our enemy's—but let not that forbid   540
Honor to Marceau![2] o'er whose early tomb
Tears, big tears, gushed from the rough soldier's lid,
Lamenting and yet envying such a doom,
Falling for France, whose rights he battled to resume.

LVII.

Brief, brave, and glorious was his young career,—   545
His mourners were two hosts, his friends and foes ;
And fitly may the stranger lingering here
Pray for his gallant spirit's bright repose ;

---

[1] Coblenz, or Koblenz, at the confluence of the Moselle with the Rhine.
[2] Marceau, a general, killed in 1796, was buried at Coblenz in the same grave as that in which his colleague, General Hoche, was laid the following year.

For he was Freedom's champion, one of those,
The few in number, who had not o'erstepped   550
The charter to chastise which she bestows
On such as wield her weapons ; he had kept
The whiteness of his soul, and thus men o'er him wept.

LVIII.

Here Ehrenbreitstein,[1] with her shattered wall
Black with the miner's blast, upon her height   555
Yet shows of what she was, when shell and ball
Rebounding idly on her strength did light:
A tower of victory! from whence the flight
Of baffled foes was watched along the plain:
But Peace destroyed what War could never blight,   560
And laid those proud roofs bare to Summer's rain—
On which the iron shower for years had poured in vain.

LIX.

Adieu to thee, fair Rhine![2]   How long delighted
The stranger fain would linger on his way!
Thine is a scene alike where souls united   565
Or lonely Contemplation thus might stray ;
And could the ceaseless vultures cease to prey
On self-condemning bosoms, it were here,
Where Nature, nor too somber nor too gay,
Wild but not rude, awful yet not austere,   570
Is to the mellow Earth as Autumn to the year.

---

[1] Ehrenbreitstein (the " Broad Stone of Honor ") is a fortified rock opposite Coblenz.
[2] Here is another transition in the poem. Byron bids adieu to the Rhine
country and presently takes the reader to the Alps. The pupil is advised to
trace the route of Harold's pilgrimage on a map. Byron gives us geography
and history in poetry.

LX.

Adieu to thee again! a vain adieu!
There can be no farewell to scene like thine;
The mind is colored by thy every hue;
And if reluctantly the eyes resign   575
Their cherished gaze upon thee, lovely Rhine!
'Tis with the thankful heart of parting praise;
More mighty spots may rise, more glaring shine,
But none unite in one attaching maze
The brilliant, fair, and soft,—the glories of old days.   580

LXI.

The negligently grand, the fruitful bloom
Of coming ripeness, the white city's sheen,
The rolling stream, the precipice's gloom,
The forest's growth, and Gothic walls between,
The wild rocks shaped as they had turrets been,   585
In mockery of man's art; and these withal
A race of faces happy as the scene,
Whose fertile bounties here extend to all,
Still springing o'er thy banks, though Empires near them fall.

LXII.

But these recede.   Above me are the Alps,[1]   590
The palaces of Nature, whose vast walls
Have pinnacled in clouds their snowy scalps,
And throned Eternity in icy halls
Of cold sublimity, where forms and falls
The avalanche—the thunderbolt of snow!   595

[1] Byron spent four months in the Alp region of Switzerland, making his
home at Coligny, near Geneva.   Much of this canto was composed at a house
called Campagna Diodati.

All that expands the spirit, yet appalls,
Gather around these summits, as to show
How Earth may pierce to Heaven, yet leave vain man below.

LXIII.

But ere these matchless heights I dare to scan,
There is a spot should not be passed in vain,—   600
Morat! the proud, the patriot field! where man
May gaze on ghastly trophies of the slain,
Nor blush for those who conquered on that plain;
Here Burgundy bequeathed his tombless host,
A bony heap, through ages to remain,   605
Themselves their monument;—the Stygian coast
Unsepulchered they roamed, and shrieked each wandering
          ghost.[1]

LXIV.

While Waterloo with Cannæ's carnage vies,
Morat and Marathon twin names shall stand;
They were true Glory's stainless victories,   610
Won by the unambitious heart and hand
Of a proud, brotherly, and civic band,
All unbought champions in no princely cause
Of vice-entailed Corruption; they no land
Doomed to bewail the blasphemy of laws   615
Making kings' rights divine, by some Draconic clause.

[1] In the battle of Morat, fought June 22, 1476, fifteen thousand men were slain, and their bones were " collected by the Swiss into an ossuary, which was destroyed in 1798." Byron, in a note, says of these bones: " A few still remain, notwithstanding the pains taken by the Burgundians for ages (all who passed that way removing a bone to their own country), and the less justifiable larcenies of the Swiss postilions, who carried them off to sell for knife handles, a purpose for which the whiteness imbibed by the bleaching of years had rendered them in great request. Of these relics I ventured to bring away as much as may have made a quarter of a hero, for which the

LXV.

By a lone wall a lonelier column rears
A gray and grief-worn aspect of old days;
'Tis the last remnant of the wreck of years,
And looks as with the wild-bewildered gaze   620
Of one to stone converted by amaze,
Yet still with consciousness; and there it stands,
Making a marvel that it not decays,
When the coeval pride of human hands,
Leveled Aventicum,[1] hath strewed her subject lands.   625

LXVI.

And there—oh! sweet and sacred be the name!—
Julia—the daughter, the devoted—gave
Her youth to Heaven; her heart, beneath a claim
Nearest to Heaven's, broke o'er a father's grave.
Justice is sworn 'gainst tears, and hers would crave   630
The life she lived in; but the judge was just,
And then she died on him she could not save.
Their tomb was simple, and without a bust,
And held within their urn one mind, one heart, one dust.[2]

sole excuse is that, if I had not, the next passer-by might have perverted them
to worse uses than the careful preservation which I intend for them."

[1] "Aventicum, near Morat, was the Roman capital of Helvetia, where
Avenches now stands" (BYRON).

[2] "Julia Alpinula, a young Aventian priestess, died soon after a vain en-
deavor to save her father, condemned to death as a traitor by Aulus Cæcina.
Her epitaph was discovered many years ago. It is thus: 'Julia Alpinula: Hic
jaceo. Infelicis patris infelix proles. Deæ Aventiæ Sacerdos. Exorare
patris necem non potui: Male mori in fatis ille erat. Vixi annos XXIII.' I
know of no human composition so affecting as this, nor a history of deeper
interest. These are the names and actions which ought not to perish"
(BYRON).

LXVII.

But these are deeds which should not pass away,   635
And names that must not wither, though the earth
Forgets her empires with a just decay,
The enslavers and the enslaved, their death and birth;
The high, the mountain majesty of worth
Should be, and shall, survivor of its woe,   640
And from its immortality look forth   ·
In the sun's face, like yonder Alpine snow,
Imperishably pure beyond all things below.

LXVIII. •

Lake Leman wooes me with its crystal face,
The mirror where the stars and mountains view   645
The stillness of their aspect in each trace
Its clear depth yields of their far height and hue:
There is too much of man here, to look through
With a fit mind the might which I behold;
But soon in me shall Loneliness renew   650
Thoughts hid, but not less cherished than of old,
Ere mingling with the herd had penned me in their fold.

LXIX.

To fly from, need not be to hate, mankind:
All are not fit with them to stir and toil,
Nor is it discontent to keep the mind   655
Deep in its fountain, lest it overboil
In the hot throng, where we become the spoil
Of our infection, till too late and long
We may deplore and struggle with the coil,
In wretched interchange of wrong for wrong   660
Midst a contentious world, striving where none are strong.

5

LXX.

There, in a moment, we may plunge our years
In fatal penitence, and in the blight
Of our own soul turn all our blood to tears,
And color things to come with hues of Night;   665
The race of life becomes a hopeless flight
To those that walk in darkness: on the sea
The boldest steer but where their ports invite;
But there are wanderers o'er Eternity
Whose bark drives on and on, and anchored ne'er shall be. 670

LXXI.

Is it not better, then, to be alone,
And love Earth only for its earthly sake?
By the blue rushing of the arrowy Rhone,[1]
Or the pure bosom of its nursing lake,
Which feeds it as a mother who doth make   675
A fair but froward infant her own care,
Kissing its cries away as these awake; —
Is it not better thus our lives to wear,
Than join the crushing crowd, doomed to inflict or bear?

LXXII.

I live not in myself, but I become   680
Portion of that around me; and to me
High mountains are a feeling, but the hum
Of human cities torture.[2]   I can see

[1] " The color of the Rhone at Geneva is blue, to a depth of tint which I
have never seen equaled in water, salt or fresh, except in the Mediterranean
and Archipelago " (BYRON).

[2] There is much here to suggest Wordsworth, as any student of Tintern
Abbey and The Excursion will discern. W. J. Rolfe quotes approvingly

Nothing to loathe in nature, save to be
A link reluctant in a fleshly chain,   685
Classed among creatures, when the soul can flee,
And with the sky, the peak, the heaving plain
Of ocean, or the stars, mingle, and not in vain.

LXXIII.

And thus I am absorbed, and this is life :
I look upon the peopled desert past,   690
As on a place of agony and strife,
Where, for some sin, to sorrow I was cast,
To act and suffer, but remount at last
With a fresh pinion ; which I feel to spring,
Though young, yet waxing vigorous as the blast   695
Which it would cope with, on delighted wing,
Spurning the clay-cold bonds which round our being cling.

LXXIV.

And when, at length, the mind shall be all free
From what it hates in this degraded form,
Reft of its carnal life, save what shall be   700
Existent happier in the fly and worm,—
When elements to elements conform,
And dust is as it should be, shall I not
Feel all I see, less dazzling, but more warm?
The bodiless thought? the Spirit of each spot?   705
Of which, even now, I share at times the immortal lot?

LXXV.

Are not the mountains, waves, and skies, a part
Of me and of my soul, as I of them?

from Dr. Darmesteter that in these lines we see '' the deep abyss between
Byron and Wordsworth: for him nature and man are enemies ; for Wordsworth they are brethren.''

Is not the love of these deep in my heart
With a pure passion; should I not contemn   710
All objects, if compared with these, and stem
A tide of suffering, rather than forego
Such feelings for the hard and worldly phlegm
Of those whose eyes are only turned below,   714
Gazing upon the ground, with thoughts which dare not glow?

LXXVI.

But this is not my theme; and I return
To that which is immediate, and require
Those who find contemplation in the urn,
To look on One,[1] whose dust was once all fire,
A native of the land where I respire   720
The clear air for a while—a passing guest,
Where he became a being,—whose desire
Was to be glorious; 'twas a foolish quest,
The which to gain and keep, he sacrificed all rest.

LXXVII.

Here the self-torturing sophist, wild Rousseau,   725
The apostle of affliction, he who threw
Enchantment over passion, and from woe
Wrung overwhelming eloquence, first drew
The breath which made him wretched; yet he knew
How to make madness beautiful, and cast   730
O'er erring deeds and thoughts a heavenly hue
Of words, like sunbeams, dazzling as they passed
The eyes, which o'er them shed tears feelingly and fast.

LXXVIII.

His love was passion's essence:—as a tree
On fire by lightning, with ethereal flame   735

---

[1] Jean Jacques Rousseau, whom commentators have compared with Byron.

Kindled he was, and blasted ; for to be
Thus, and enamored, were in him the same.
But his was not the love of living dame,
Nor of the dead who rise upon our dreams,
But of ideal beauty, which became   740
In him existence, and o'erflowing teems
Along his burning page, distempered though it seems.

LXXIX.

This breathed itself to life in Julie,[1] *this*
Invested her with all that's wild and sweet ;
This hallowed, too, the memorable kiss   745
Which every morn his fevered lip would greet,
From hers, who but with friendship his would meet ;
But to that gentle touch through brain and breast
Flashed the thrilled spirit's love-devouring heat ;
In that absorbing sigh perchance more blessed   750
Than vulgar minds may be with all they seek possessed.

LXXX.

His life was one long war with self-sought foes,
Or friends by him self-banished ; for his mind
Had grown Suspicion's sanctuary,[2] and chose,
For its own cruel sacrifice, the kind,   755
'Gainst whom he raged with fury strange and blind.
But he was frenzied,—wherefore, who may know,
Since cause might be which skill could never find?
But he was frenzied by disease or woe,
To that worst pitch of all, which wears a reasoning show. 760

----

[1] The Comtesse d'Houdetot, whom Rousseau loved.
[2] Carlyle relates that to a visitor Rousseau said " with flaming eyes " : " I
know why you come here. You come to see what a poor life I lead, how
little is in my poor pot that is boiling there."

LXXXI.

For then he was inspired, and from him came,
As from the Pythian's mystic cave of yore,
Those oracles which set the world in flame,
Nor ceased to burn till kingdoms were no more :
Did he not this for France [1] which lay before   765
Bowed to the inborn tyranny of years,
Broken and trembling to the yoke she bore,
Till by the voice of him and his compeers
Roused up to too much wrath, which follows o'ergrown fears?

LXXXII.

They made themselves a fearful monument!   770
The wreck of old opinions—things which grew,
Breathed from the birth of time : the veil they rent,
And what behind it lay, all earth shall view.
But good with ill they also overthrew,
Leaving but ruins, wherewith to rebuild   775
Upon the same foundation, and renew
Dungeons and thrones, which the same hour refilled,
As heretofore, because ambition was self-willed.

LXXXIII.

But this will not endure, nor be endured!
Mankind have felt their strength, and made it felt.   780
They might have used it better, but, allured
By their new vigor, sternly have they dealt
On one another ; pity ceased to melt
With her once natural charities.   But they,

---

[1] " No writer of the eighteenth century was so influential in bringing
about the French Revolution as Rousseau " (TOZER).

Who in oppression's darkness caved had dwelt,   785
They were not eagles, nourished with the day;
What marvel then, at times, if they mistook their prey? [1]

LXXXIV.

What deep wounds ever closed without a scar?
The heart's bleed longest, and but heal to wear
That which disfigures it; and they who war   790
With their own hopes, and have been vanquished, bear
Silence, but not submission: in his lair
Fixed Passion holds his breath, until the hour
Which shall atone for years; none need despair:
It came, it cometh, and will come,—the power   795
To punish or forgive—in *one* we shall be slower.

LXXXV.

Clear, placid Leman! thy contrasted lake,
With the wild world I dwelt in, is a thing
Which warns me, with its stillness, to forsake
Earth's troubled waters for a purer spring.   800
This quiet sail is as a noiseless wing [2]
To waft me from distraction; once I loved
Torn ocean's roar, but thy soft murmuring
Sounds sweet as if a Sister's voice reproved,
That I with stern delights should e'er have been so moved. 805

---

[1] Teachers might add interest to the study of this passage in the poem by commenting on Byron's opinion of the French Revolution and by presenting other views from different authors.

[2] Byron and Shelley sailed round and across Lake Geneva in a small boat in the last days of June, 1816. This excursion furnished Byron material for the charming stanzas that follow. Rolfe remarks that these stanzas " have a harmony and a sweetness that is like Shelley." Professor Keene notes that " in this lovely passage the charms of the calm are enhanced as a skillful preparation for what is coming."

LXXXVI.

It is the hush of night, and all between
Thy margin and the mountains, dusk, yet clear,
Mellowed and mingling, yet distinctly seen,
Save darkened Jura, whose capped heights appear
Precipitously steep; and drawing near,   810
There breathes a living fragrance from the shore,
Of flowers yet fresh with childhood;[1] on the ear
Drops the light drip of the suspended oar,
Or chirps the grasshopper one good-night carol more;

LXXXVII.

He is an evening reveler, who makes   815
His life an infancy, and sings his fill;
At intervals, some bird from out the brakes
Starts into voice a moment, then is still.
There seems a floating whisper on the hill,
But that is fancy, for the starlight dews   820
All silently their tears of love instill,
Weeping themselves away, till they infuse
Deep into Nature's breast the spirit of her hues.

LXXXVIII.

Ye stars! which are the poetry of heaven!
If in your bright leaves we would read the fate   825
Of men and empires,—'tis to be forgiven
That, in our aspirations to be great,
Our destinies o'erleap their mortal state,
And claim a kindred with you; for ye are

---

[1] " Notice the beautiful pause after the seventh syllable, which is frequent in this part of the poem, as in lines 792, 802, 829, 849, 863 " (TOZER).

A beauty and a mystery, and create   830
In us such love and reverence from afar,
That fortune, fame, power, life, have named themselves a star.

LXXXIX.

All heaven and earth are still—though not in sleep,
But breathless, as we grow when feeling most;
And silent, as we stand in thoughts too deep:—   835
All heaven and earth are still: From the high host
Of stars to the lulled lake and mountain coast,
All is concentered in a life intense,
Where not a beam, nor air, nor leaf is lost,
But hath a part of being, and a sense   840
Of that which is of all Creator and defense.

XC.

Then stirs the feeling infinite, so felt
In solitude, where we are *least* alone;
A truth, which through our being then doth melt,
And purifies from self: it is a tone,   845
The soul and source of music, which makes known
Eternal harmony, and sheds a charm
Like to the fabled Cytherea's zone,[1]
Binding all things with beauty;—'twould disarm
The specter Death, had he substantial power to harm.   850

XCI.

Not vainly did the early Persian make
His altar the high places, and the peak
Of earth-o'ergazing mountains, and thus take
A fit and unwalled temple, there to seek

[1] The zone or girdle of Venus, " which had the power of inspiring love for the wearer."

The Spirit, in whose honor shrines are weak,   855
Upreared of human hands.   Come, and compare
Columns and idol dwellings, Goth or Greek,
With Nature's realms of worship, earth and air,
Nor fix on fond abodes to circumscribe thy pray'r![1]

XCII.

The sky is changed! —and such a change!   O night,   860
And storm, and darkness, ye are wondrous strong,
Yet lovely in your strength, as is the light
Of a dark eye in woman!   Far along,
From peak to peak, the rattling crags among
Leaps the live thunder!   Not from one lone cloud,   865
But every mountain now hath found a tongue,
And Jura answers, through her misty shroud,
Back to the joyous Alps, who call to her aloud![2]

XCIII.

And this is in the night:—Most glorious night!
Thou wert not sent for slumber! let me be   870
A sharer in thy fierce and far delight,—
A portion of the tempest and of thee!
How the lit lake shines, a phosphoric sea,
And the big rain comes dancing to the earth!

---

[1] "The groves were God's first temples" (BRYANT).

> "Go thou and seek the house of prayer;
> I to the woodlands will repair
> And seek the God of nature there."
>   SOUTHEY.

[2] "The thunderstorm to which these lines refer occurred on the 13th of June, 1816, at midnight.   I have seen among the mountains several more terrible, but none more beautiful" (BYRON).

And now again 'tis black,—and now the glee   875
Of the loud hills shakes with its mountain mirth,
As if they did rejoice o'er a young earthquake's birth.

XCIV.

Now, where the swift Rhone cleaves his way between
Heights which appear as lovers who have parted
In hate, whose mining depths so intervene,   880
That they can meet no more, though broken-hearted;
Though in their souls, which thus each other thwarted,
Love was the very root of the fond rage
Which blighted their life's bloom, and then departed:
Itself expired, but leaving them an age   885
Of years all winters,—war within themselves to wage.

XCV.

Now, where the quick Rhone thus hath cleft his way,
The mightiest of the storms hath ta'en his stand:
For here, not one, but many, make their play,
And fling their thunderbolts from hand to hand,   890
Flashing and cast around; of all the band,
The brightest through these parted hills hath forked
His lightnings,—as if he did understand
That in such gaps as desolation worked,
There the hot shaft should blast whatever therein lurked. 895

XCVI.

Sky, mountains, river, winds, lake, lightnings! ye!
With night, and clouds, and thunder, and a soul
To make these felt and feeling, well may be
. Things that have made me watchful; the far roll
Of your departing voices is the knoll   900
Of what in me is sleepless,—if I rest.

But where of ye, O tempests! is the goal?
Are ye like those within the human breast?
Or do ye find, at length, like eagles, some high nest?

XCVII.

Could I embody and unbosom now   905
That which is most within me,—could I wreak
My thoughts upon expression, and thus throw
Soul, heart, mind, passions, feelings, strong or weak,
All that I would have sought, and all I seek,
Bear, know, feel, and yet breathe—into *one* word,   910
And that one word were Lightning, I would speak ;
But as it is, I live and die unheard,
With a most voiceless thought, sheathing it as a sword.

XCVIII.

The morn is up again, the dewy morn,
With breath all incense, and with cheek all bloom,   915
Laughing the clouds away with playful scorn,
And living as if earth contained no tomb,—
And glowing into day : we may resume
The march of our existence : and thus I,
Still on thy shores, fair Leman! may find room   920
And food for meditation, nor pass by
Much, that may give us pause, if pondered fittingly.

XCIX.

Clarens![1] sweet Clarens, birthplace of deep Love!
Thine air is the young breath of passionate thought ;

---

[1] A village near Vevay, on Lake Geneva. Rousseau has described it in
his writings. In a long note Byron says: "It would be difficult to see
Clarens (with the scenes around it,—Vevay, Chillon, Bôveret, Saint-Gingo,

Thy trees take root in Love; the snows above 925
The very Glaciers have his colors caught,
And sunset into rose hues sees them wrought
By rays which sleep there lovingly: the rocks,
The permanent crags, tell here of Love, wh●sought
In them a refuge from the worldly shocks, 930
Which stir and sting the soul with hope that wooes, then mocks.

C.

Clarens! by heavenly feet thy paths are trod,—
Undying Love's, who here ascends a throne
To which the steps are mountains; where the god
Is a pervading life and light,—so shown 935
Not on those summits solely, nor alone
In the still cave and forest; o'er the flower
His eye is sparkling, and his breath hath blown,
His soft and summer breath, whose tender power
Passes the strength of storms in their most desolate hour. 940

CI.

All things are here of *him;* from the black pines,
Which are his shade on high, and the loud roar
Of torrents, where he listeneth, to the vines
Which slope his green path downward to the shore,
Where the bowed waters meet him, and adore, 945
Kissing his feet with murmurs; and the wood,
The covert of old trees, with trunks all hoar,
But light leaves, young as joy, stands where it stood,
Offering to him, and his, a populous solitude.

Meillerie, Eivan, and the entrances of the Rhone) without being forcibly
struck with its peculiar adaptation to the persons and events with which it
has been peopled."

CII.

A populous solitude of bees and birds,   950
And fairy-formed and many-colored things,
Who worship him with notes more sweet than words,
And innocently open their glad wings,
Fearless and full of life: the gush of springs,
And fall of lofty fountains, and the bend   955
Of stirring branches, and the bud which brings
The swiftest thought of beauty, here extend,
Mingling, and made by Love, unto one mighty end.

CIII.

He who hath loved not, here would learn that lore,
And make his heart a spirit; he who knows   960
That tender mystery, will love the more;
For this is Love's recess, where vain men's woes,
And the world's waste, have driven him far from those,
For 'tis his nature to advance or die;
He stands not still, but or decays, or grows   965
Into a boundless blessing, which may vie
With the immortal lights, in its eternity!

CIV.

'Twas not for fiction chose Rousseau this spot,
Peopling it with affections; but he found
It was the scene which Passion must allot   970
To the mind's purified beings; 'twas the ground
Where early Love his Psyche's [1] zone unbound,
And hallowed it with loveliness: 'tis lone,
And wonderful, and deep, and hath a sound,
And sense, and sight of sweetness; here the Rhone   975
Hath spread himself a couch, the Alps have reared a throne.

[1] Read the myth of Cupid and Psyche.

CV.

Lausanne![1] and Ferney![2] ye have been the abodes
Of names which unto you bequeathed a name;
Mortals, who sought and found, by dangerous roads,
A path to perpetuity of fame: 980
They were gigantic minds, and their steep aim
Was, Titan-like, on daring doubts to pile
Thoughts which should call down thunder, and the flame
Of Heaven, again assailed, if Heaven the while   984
On man and man's research could deign do more than smile.

CVI.

The one [3] was fire and fickleness, a child
Most mutable in wishes, but in mind
A wit as various,—gay, grave, sage, or wild,—
Historian, bard, philosopher, combined;
He multiplied himself among mankind,   990
The Proteus of their talents: But his own
Breathed most in ridicule,—which, as the wind,
Blew where it listed, laying all things prone,—
Now to o'erthrow a fool, and now to shake a throne.

CVII.

The other,[4] deep and slow, exhausting thought,   995
And hiving wisdom with each studious year,
In meditation dwelt, with learning wrought,
And shaped his weapon with an edge severe,
Sapping a solemn creed with solemn sneer; [4]
The lord of irony,—that master spell,   1000

[1] Lausanne is on the north side of Lake Geneva. In a letter to Thomas
Moore, Shelley wrote: " We visited Lausanne, and saw Gibbon's house.
We were shown the decayed summerhouse where he finished his history."
[2] Ferney, near Geneva, was the home of Voltaire.   [3] Voltaire.
[4] Gibbon attacked Christianity in The Decline and Fall of the Roman Empire.

Which stung his foes to wrath, which grew from fear,
And doomed him to the zealot's ready Hell,
Which answers to all doubts so eloquently well.

CVIII.

Yet, peace be with their ashes,—for by them,
If merited, the penalty is paid;   1005
It is not ours to judge, far less condemn;
The hour must come when such things shall be made
Known unto all,—or hope and dread allayed
By slumber, on one pillow, in the dust,
Which, thus much we are sure, must lie decayed;   1010
And when it shall revive, as is our trust,
'Twill be to be forgiven, or suffer what is just.

CIX.

But let me quit man's works, again to read
His Maker's, spread around me, and suspend
This page, which from my reveries I feed,   1015
Until it seems prolonging without end.
The clouds above me to the white Alps tend,
And I must pierce them, and survey whate'er
May be permitted, as my steps I bend
To their most great and growing region, where   1020
The earth to her embrace compels the powers of air.

CX.

Italia! too, Italia! looking on thee,
Full flashes on the soul the light of ages,
Since the fierce Carthaginian almost won thee,
To the last halo of the chiefs and sages   1025
Who glorify thy consecrated pages;
Thou wert the throne and grave of empires; still,

The fount at which the panting mind assuages
Her thirst of knowledge, quaffing there her fill,
Flows from the eternal source of Rome's imperial hill.[1]   1030

CXI.

Thus far have I proceeded in a theme
Renewed with no kind auspices: —to feel
We are not what we have been, and to deem
We are not what we should be, and to steel
The heart against itself; and to conceal,   1035
With a proud caution, love, or hate, or aught,—
Passion or feeling, purpose, grief, or zeal,—
Which is the tyrant spirit of our thought,
Is a stern task of soul: —No matter,—it is taught.

CXII.

And for these words, thus woven into song,   1040
It may be that they are a harmless wile,—
The coloring of the scenes which fleet along,
Which I would seize. in passing, to beguile
My breast, or that of others, for a while.
Fame is the thirst of youth, but I am not   1045
So young as to regard men's frown or smile,
As loss or guerdon of a glorious lot;
I stood and stand alone,—remembered or forgot.

CXIII.

I have not loved the world, nor the world me;
I have not flattered its rank breath, nor bowed   1050
To its idolatries a patient knee,
Nor coined my cheek to smiles, nor cried aloud

[1] Byron resumes the subject of Italy in the fourth canto.

6

In worship of an echo; in the crowd
They could not deem me one of such; I stood
Among them, but not of them; in a shroud   1055
Of thoughts which were not their thoughts, and still could,
Had I not filed my mind,[1] which thus itself subdued.

CXIV.

I have not loved the world, nor the world me,—
But let us part fair foes; I do believe,
Though I have found them not, that there may be   1060
Words which are things,[2] hopes which will not deceive,
And virtues which are merciful, nor weave
Snares for the failing; I would also deem
O'er others' griefs that some sincerely grieve;
That two, or one, are almost what they seem,—   1065
That goodness is no name, and happiness no dream.

CXV.

My daughter! with thy name this song begun;
My daughter! with thy name thus much shall end;
I see thee not, I hear thee not, but none
Can be so wrapt in thee; thou art the friend   1070
To whom the shadows of far years extend:
Albeit my brow thou never shouldst behold,
My voice shall with thy future visions blend,
And reach into thy heart, when mine is cold,
A token and a tone, even from thy father's mold.   1075

[1] Defiled. " For Banquo's issue have I filed my mind " (Macbeth, iii. i.).

[2] " But words are things, and a small drop of ink
        Falling, like dew, upon a thought, produces
        That which makes thousands, perhaps millions, think."
                                        BYRON's *Don Juan.*

CXVI.

To aid thy mind's development, to watch
Thy dawn of little joys, to sit and see
Almost thy very growth, to view thee catch
Knowledge of objects,—wonders yet to thee!
To hold thee lightly on a gentle knee,   1080
And print on thy soft cheek a parent's kiss,—
This, it should seem, was not reserved for me ;
Yet this was in my nature: as it is,
I know not what is there, yet something like to this.

CXVII.

Yet, though dull Hate as duty should be taught,   1085
I know that thou wilt love me ; though my name
Should be shut from thee, as a spell still fraught
With desolation, and a broken claim :
Though the grave closed between us,—'twere the same,
I know that thou wilt love me ; though to drain   1090
My blood from out.thy being were an aim,
And an attainment,—all would be in vain,—
Still thou wouldst love me, still that more than life retain.

CXVIII.

The child of love, though born in bitterness,
And nurtured in convulsion.   Of thy sire   1095
These were the elements, and thine no less.
As yet such are around thee, but thy fire
Shall be more tempered, and thy hope far higher.
Sweet be thy cradled slumbers!   O'er the sea
And from the mountains where I now respire,   1100
Fain would I waft such blessing upon thee,
As, with a sigh, I deem thou mightst have been to me.

CANTO THE FOURTH.[1]

" Visto ho Toscana, Lombardia, Romagna,
    Quel Monte che divide, e quel che serra
Italia, e un mare e l' altro, che la bagna."[2]
                    ARIOSTO, *Satira iii.*

I.

I stood in Venice, on the Bridge of Sighs;[3]
A palace and a prison on each hand:
I saw from out the wave her structures rise
As from the stroke of the enchanter's wand:
A thousand years their cloudy wings expand   5
Around me, and a dying Glory smiles
O'er the far times, when many a subject land
Looked to the wingèd Lion's marble piles,
Where Venice sate in state, throned on her hundred isles!

II.

She looks a sea Cybele,[4] fresh from ocean,   10
Rising with her tiara of proud towers

---

[1] This canto was begun at Venice in June, 1817, and was published early
in 1818, with an introductory letter to the poet's friend and traveling companion, Hobhouse, who furnished ample historical notes for it.

[2] "I have seen Tuscany, Lombardy, and the Romagna, the mountain
ranges which divide and those which border Italy, and the one sea and the
other which bathe her."

[3] Across which prisoners were conducted from the palace to the prison.

[4] The goddess of the earth.

84

At airy distance, with majestic motion,
A ruler of the waters and their powers:
And such she was;—her daughters had their dowers
From spoils of nations, and the exhaustless East   15
Poured in her lap all gems in sparkling showers.
In purple was she robed, and of her feast
Monarchs partook, and deemed their dignity increased.

III.

In Venice Tasso's echoes are no more,
And silent rows the songless gondolier;   20
Her palaces are crumbling to the shore,
And music meets not always now the ear:
Those days are gone—but Beauty still is here.
States fall, arts fade—but Nature doth not die,
Nor yet forget how Venice once was dear,   25
The pleasant place of all festivity,
The revel of the earth, the mask of Italy!

IV.

But unto us she hath a spell beyond
Her name in story, and her long array
· Of mighty shadows, whose dim forms despond   30
Above the dogeless city's vanished sway;
Ours is a trophy which will not decay
With the Rialto;[1] Shylock and the Moor,
And Pierre, cannot be swept or worn away[2]—
The keystones of the arch! though all were o'er,   35
For us repeopled were the solitary shore.

---

[1] A bridge spanning the Grand Canal, Venice.
[2] See Shakespeare's Merchant of Venice and Othello the Moor of Venice;
also Otway's Venice Preserved.

V.

The beings of the mind are not of clay;
Essentially immortal, they create
And multiply in us a brighter ray
And more beloved existence: that which Fate   40
Prohibits to dull life, in this our state
Of mortal bondage, by these spirits supplied,
First exiles, then replaces what we hate;
Watering the heart whose early flowers have died,
And with a fresher growth replenishing the void.   45

VI.

Such is the refuge of our youth and age,
The first from Hope, the last from Vacancy;
And this worn feeling peoples many a page,
And, maybe, that which grows beneath mine eye:
Yet there are things whose strong reality   50
Outshines our fairyland; in shape and hues
More beautiful than our fantastic sky,
And the strange constellations which the Muse
O'er her wild universe is skillful to diffuse:

VII.

I saw or dreamed of such,—but let them go,—   55
They came like truth, and disappeared like dreams;
And whatsoe'er they were—are now but so:
I could replace them if I would; still teems
My mind with many a form which aptly seems
Such as I sought for, and at moments found;   60
Let these too go—for waking Reason deems
Such overweening fantasies unsound,
And other voices speak, and other sights surround.

VIII.

I've taught me other tongues,[1] and in strange eyes
Have made me not a stranger; to the mind   65
Which is itself, no changes bring surprise;
Nor is it harsh to make, nor hard to find
A country with—aye, or without mankind;
Yet was I born where men are proud to be,—
Not without cause; and should I leave behind   70
The inviolate island of the sage and free,[2]
And seek me out a home by a remoter sea,

IX.

Perhaps I loved it well: and should I lay
My ashes in a soil which is not mine,
My spirit shall resume it—if we may   75
Unbodied choose a sanctuary. I twine
My hopes of being remembered in my line
With my land's language: if too fond and far
These aspirations in their scope incline,—
If my fame should be, as my fortunes are,   80
Of hasty growth and blight, and dull Oblivion bar

. X.

My name from out the temple where the dead
Are honored by the nations—let it be—
And light the laurels on a loftier head!
And be the Spartan's epitaph on me—   85
"Sparta hath many a worthier son than he."
Meantime I seek no sympathies, nor need;

---

[1] Byron was familiar with the Italian language.
[2] What island is meant?

The thorns which I have reaped are of the tree
I planted: they have torn me, and I bleed: 89
I should have known what fruit would spring from such a seed.

XI.

The spouseless Adriatic mourns her lord;[1]
And, annual marriage now no more renewed,
The Bucentaur lies rotting unrestored,
Neglected garment of her widowhood!
St. Mark yet sees his lion where he stood[2]   95
Stand, but in mockery of his withered power,
Over the proud Place where an Emperor sued,
And monarchs gazed and envied in the hour
When Venice was a queen with an unequaled dower.

XII.

The Suabian[3] sued, and now the Austrian reigns—   100
An Emperor[4] tramples where an Emperor knelt;
Kingdoms are shrunk to provinces, and chains
Clank over sceptered cities; nations melt
From power's high pinnacle, when they have felt
The sunshine for a while, and downward go   105
Like lauwine[5] loosened from the mountain's belt;
Oh for one hour of blind old Dandolo![6]
Th' octogenarian chief, Byzantium's conquering foe.

---

[1] The doge of Venice used to "wed the Adriatic" by dropping a ring into the sea annually, on Ascension Day, to indicate that he was lord of the waters.

[2] The patron saint of Venice. The winged lion of St. Mark is on a column at the entrance of the Piazzetta, the "proud Place" where Barbarossa the emperor bowed to the pope in 1177.

[3] Barbarossa.   [4] Napoleon.   [5] Avalanche.

[6] The doge who, in 1204, led the assault on Constantinople.

XIII.

Before St. Mark still glow his steeds of brass,
Their gilded collars glittering in the sun;[1]   110
But is not Doria's[2] menace come to pass?
Are they not *bridled?* — Venice, lost and won,
Her thirteen hundred years of freedom done,
Sinks, like a seaweed, into whence she rose!
Better be whelmed beneath the waves, and shun,   115
Even in destruction's depth, her foreign foes,
From whom submission wrings an infamous repose.

XIV.

In youth she was all glory,—a new Tyre;
Her very byword sprung from victory,
The " Planter of the Lion,"[3] which through fire   120
And blood she bore o'er subject earth and sea;
Though making many slaves, herself still free,
And Europe's bulwark 'gainst the Ottomite;
Witness Troy's rival, Candia![4] Vouch it, ye
Immortal waves that saw Lepanto's fight![5]   125
For ye are names no time nor tyranny can blight.

· XV. .

Statues of glass—all shivered—the long file
Of her dead Doges are declined to dust;

---

[1] " The famous bronze horses above the portal of St. Mark's Church. Constantine carried them from Rome to Constantinople, whence Dandolo brought them to Venice. In 1797 Napoleon took them to Paris, but in 1815 they were restored to their former position in Venice " (ROLFE).

[2] A Genoese commander who threatened to bridle the horses.

[3] " The lion of St. Mark, the standard of the republic " (BYRON).

[4] Candia, the capital of Crete, held out against a siege of twenty-four years, while Troy was taken in ten years.

[5] The Turks were defeated near the entrance of the Strait of Lepanto.

But where they dwelt, the vast and sumptuous pile
Bespeaks the pageant of their splendid trust;   130
Their scepter broken, and their sword in rust,
Have yielded to the stranger: empty halls,
Thin streets, and foreign aspects, such as must
Too oft remind her who and what inthralls,
Have flung a desolate cloud o'er Venice' lovely walls.   135

XVI.

When Athens' armies fell at Syracuse,
And fettered thousands bore the yoke of war,
Redemption rose up in the Attic Muse,
Her voice their only ransom from afar:[1]
See! as they chant the tragic hymn, the car   140
Of the o'ermastered victor stops, the reins
Fall from his hands, his idle scimiter
Starts from its belt—he rends his captive's chains,
And bids him thank the bard for freedom and his strains.

XVII.

Thus, Venice, if no stronger claim were thine,   145
Were all thy proud historic deeds forgot,
Thy choral memory of the Bard divine,
Thy love of Tasso, should have cut the knot
Which ties thee to thy tyrants; and thy lot
Is shameful to the nations,—most of all,   150
Albion![2] to thee: the Ocean queen should not
Abandon Ocean's children; in the fall
Of Venice think of thine, despite thy watery wall.

---

[1] Read, in Plutarch's Life of Nicias, how certain Greek captives ransomed themselves by reciting Attic poetry. (See Browning's Balaustion's Adventure.)
[2] England.

XVIII.

I loved her from my boyhood; she to me
Was as a fairy city of the heart,   155
Rising like water columns from the sea,
Of joy the sojourn, and of wealth the mart;
And Otway, Radcliffe,[1] Schiller,[1] Shakespeare's art,
Had stamped her image in me, and even so,
Although I found her thus, we did not part;   160
Perchance even dearer in her day of woe,
Than when she was a boast, a marvel, and a show.

XIX.

I can repeople with the past—and of
The present there is still for eye and thought,
And meditation chastened down, enough;   165
And more, it may be, than I hoped or sought;
And of the happiest moments which were wrought
Within the web of my existence, some
From thee, fair Venice! have their colors caught:
There are some feelings Time cannot benumb,   170
Nor Torture shake, or mine would now be cold and dumb.

XX.

But from their nature will the tannen[2] grow
Loftiest on loftiest and least sheltered rocks,
Rooted in barrenness, where naught below
Of soil supports them 'gainst the Alpine shocks   175
Of eddying storms; yet springs the trunk, and mocks
The howling tempest, till its height and frame

[1] Ann Radcliffe wrote The Mysteries of Udolpho.   J. C. F. Schiller wrote
The Ghost Seer.   These books relate to Italy.
[2] The plural of the German *Tanne,* a fir tree.

Are worthy of the mountains from whose blocks
Of bleak, gray granite into life it came,
And grew a giant tree;—the mind may grow the same.   180

XXI.

Existence may be borne, and the deep root
Of life and sufferance make its firm abode
The bare and desolated bosoms: mute
The camel labors with the heaviest load,
And the wolf dies in silence,—not bestowed   185
In vain should such example be; if they,
Things of ignoble or of savage mood,
Endure and shrink not, we of nobler clay
May temper it to bear,—it is but for a day.

XXII.

All suffering doth destroy, or is destroyed,   190
Even by the sufferer; and, in each event,
Ends: Some, with hope replenished and rebuoyed,
Return to whence they came—with like intent,
And weave their web again; some, bowed and bent,
Wax gray and ghastly, withering ere their time,   195
And perish with the reed on which they leant;
Some seek devotion, toil, war, good or crime,
According as their souls were formed to sink or climb.

XXIII.

But ever and anon of griefs subdued
There comes a token like a scorpion's sting,   200
Scarce seen, but with fresh bitterness imbued;
And slight withal may be the things which bring
Back on the heart the weight which it would fling
Aside forever: it may be a sound—

A tone of music—summer's eve—or spring— 205
A flower—the wind—the ocean—which shall wound,
Striking the electric chain wherewith we are darkly bound;

XXIV.

And how and why we know not, nor can trace
Home to its cloud this lightning of the mind,
But feel the shock renewed, nor can efface 210
The blight and blackening which it leaves behind,
Which out of things familiar, undesigned,
When least we deem of such, calls up to view
The specters whom no exorcism can bind,—
The cold, the changed, perchance the dead—anew, 215
The mourned, the loved, the lost—too many! yet how few!

XXV.[1]

But my soul wanders; I demand it back
To meditate amongst decay, and stand
A ruin amidst ruins; there to track
Fall'n states and buried greatness, o'er a land 220
Which *was* the mightiest in its old command,
And *is* the loveliest, and must ever be
The master mold of Nature's heavenly hand;
Wherein were cast the heroic and the free,
The beautiful, the brave, the lords of earth and sea, 225

XXVI.[2]

The commonwealth of kings, the men of Rome!
And even since, and now, fair Italy!

[1] Byron here begins the poetical record of a six weeks' tour through northern Italy. He left Venice in April, 1817, and returned late in May.

[2] Professor Keene singles out this stanza as "a passage of high feeling couched in faultless language."

Thou art the garden of the world, the home
Of all Art yields, and Nature can decree;
Even in thy desert, what is like to thee?   230
Thy very weeds are beautiful, thy waste
More rich than other climes' fertility;
Thy wreck a glory, and thy ruin graced
With an immaculate charm which cannot be defaced.

XXVII.[1]

The moon is up, and yet it is not night;   235
Sunset divides the sky with her; a sea
Of glory streams along the Alpine height
Of blue Friuli's[2] mountains.   Heaven is free
From clouds, but of all colors seems to be,—
Melted to one vast Iris of the West,—   240
Where the Day joins the past Eternity,
While, on the other hand, meek Dian's crest[3]
Floats through the azure air—an island of the blest!

XXVIII.

A single star is at her side,[4] and reigns
With her o'er half the lovely heaven; but still   245
Yon sunny sea heaves brightly, and remains
Rolled o'er the peak of the far Rhætian hill,
As Day and Night contending were, until
Nature reclaimed her order:—gently flows

---

[1] Professor Tozer says: "This description of sunset is the nearest approach to word painting that can be found in the poem."
  [2] The Julian Alps.   [3] The crescent moon.

      [4] " The horned moon, with one bright star
          Within the nether tip."
              COLERIDGE'S *Ancient Mariner.*

The deep-dyed Brenta, where their hues instill　　250
The odorous purple of a new-born rose,
Which streams upon her stream, and glassed within it glows,

XXIX.

Filled with the face of heaven, which, from afar,
Comes down upon the waters; all its hues,
From the rich sunset to the rising star,　　255
Their magical variety diffuse :
And now they change; a paler shadow strews
Its mantle o'er the mountains; parting day
Dies like the dolphin, whom each pang imbues
With a new color as it gasps away,　　260
The last still loveliest,—till—'tis gone—and all is gray.

XXX.

There is a tomb in Arqua;[1]—reared in air,
Pillared in their sarcophagus, repose
The bones of Laura's[2] lover: here repair
Many familiar with his well-sung woes,　　265
The pilgrims of his genius.　He arose
To raise a language, and his land reclaim
From the dull yoke of her barbaric foes :
Watering the tree which bears his lady's name
With his melodious tears, he gave himself to fame.　　270

XXXI.

They keep his dust in Arqua, where he died ;
The mountain village where his latter days

---

[1] A village in which the Italian poet Petrarch died, July 18, 1374.　His
house still stands, and his tomb, a sarcophagus resting on pillars of red marble, is visited by many tourists.

[2] Laura, a lady of Avignon, whom Petrarch loved and to whom he
addressed many of his sonnets.

Went down the vale of years; and 'tis their pride—
An honest pride—and let it be their praise,
To offer to the passing stranger's gaze   275
His mansion and his sepulcher; both plain
And venerably simple, such as raise
A feeling more accordant with his strain
Than if a pyramid formed his monumental fane.

XXXII.

And the soft, quiet hamlet where he dwelt   280
Is one of that complexion [1] which seems made
For those who their mortality have felt,
And sought a refuge from their hopes decayed
In the deep umbrage of a green hill's shade,
Which shows a distant prospect far away   285
Of busy cities, now in vain displayed,·
For they can lure no further; and the ray
Of a bright sun can make sufficient holiday,

XXXIII.

Developing the mountains, leaves, and flowers,
And shining in the brawling brook, whereby,   290
Clear as its current, glide the sauntering hours
With a calm languor, which, though to the eye
Idlesse [2] it seem, hath its morality.
If from society we learn to live,
'Tis solitude should teach us how to die; [3]   295
It hath no flatterers; vanity can give
No hollow aid; alone—man with his God must strive:

[1] Study the meanings of the word "complexion."
[2] Archaic form for "idleness."
[3] "How blest the Solitary's lot" (ROBERT BURNS).

XXXIV.

Or, it may be, with demons,[1] who impair
The strength of better thoughts, and seek their prey
In melancholy bosoms, such as were   300
Of moody texture from their earliest day,
And loved to dwell in darkness and dismay,
Deeming themselves predestined to a doom
Which is not of the pangs that pass away;
Making the sun like blood, the earth a tomb,   305
The tomb a hell, and hell itself a murkier gloom.

XXXV.

Ferrara![2] in thy wide and grass-grown streets,
Whose symmetry was not for solitude,
There seems as 'twere a curse upon the seats
Of former sovereigns, and the antique brood   310
Of Este,[3] which for many an age made good
Its strength within thy walls, and was of yore
Patron or tyrant, as the changing mood
Of petty power impelled, of those who wore
The wreath which Dante's brow alone had worn before. 315

XXXVI.

And Tasso[4] is their glory and their shame.
Hark to his strain! and then survey his cell!

---

[1] "The struggle is to the full as likely to be with demons as with our better thoughts.   Satan chose the wilderness for the temptation of our Savior; and our unsullied John Locke preferred the presence of a child to complete solitude" (BYRON).   [2] Once an important town.

[3] A noble Italian family.   (See Browning's *Sordello*.)

[4] Tasso's great poem is called *Jerusalem Delivered*.   (See Byron's Lament of Tasso.)

7

And see how dearly earned Torquato's fame,
And where Alfonso [1] bade his poet dwell:
The miserable despot could not quell   320
The insulted mind he sought to quench, and blend
With the surrounding maniacs, in the hell
Where he had plunged it.   Glory without end
Scattered the clouds away; and on that name attend

XXXVII.

The tears and praises of all time; while thine   325
Would rot in its oblivion—in the sink
Of worthless dust, which from thy boasted line
Is shaken into nothing—but the link
Thou formest in his fortunes bids us think
Of thy poor malice, naming thee with scorn: 330
Alfonso! how thy ducal pageants shrink
From thee! if in another station born,
Scarce fit to be the slave of him thou madest to mourn:

XXXVIII.

Thou ! formed to eat, and be despised, and die,
Even as the beasts that perish, save that thou   335
Hadst a more splendid trough and wider sty:
He ! with a glory round his furrowed brow,
Which emanated then, and dazzles now,
In face of all his foes, the Cruscan quire,[2]
And Boileau,[3] whose rash envy could allow   340
No strain which shamed his country's creaking lyre,
That whetstone of the teeth—monotony in wire!

[1] Duke of Ferrara, who imprisoned Tasso as being a madman, because
the poet dared to love the duke's sister.
[2] A Florentine literary society, Della Crusca, or " Academy of Chaff."
[3] A French critic who underrated Tasso's poetry.

XXXIX.

Peace to Torquato's injured shade! 'twas his
In life and death to be the mark where Wrong
Aimed with her poisoned arrows,—but to miss.   345
Oh, victor unsurpassed in modern song!
Each year brings forth its millions; but how long
The tide of generations shall roll on,
And not the whole combined and countless throng
Compose a mind like thine? though all in one   350
Condensed their scattered rays, they would not form a sun.

XL.

Great as thou art, yet paralleled by those,
Thy countrymen, before thee born to shine,
The Bards of Hell and Chivalry :[1] first rose
The Tuscan father's comedy divine ;   355
Then, not unequal to the Florentine,
The southern Scott, the minstrel who called forth
A new creation with his magic line,
And, like the Ariosto of the North,
Sang ladye love and war, romance and knightly worth.   360

XLI.

The lightning rent from Ariosto's bust
The iron crown of laurel's mimicked leaves ;
Nor was the ominous element unjust,
For the true laurel wreath which Glory weaves
Is of the tree no bolt of thunder cleaves,   365
And the false semblance but disgraced his brow ;

---

[1] Dante and Ariosto. The first part of Dante's greatest poem is called
Inferno. Ariosto's Orlando Furioso is largely a poem of chivalry.

Yet still, if fondly Superstition grieves,
Know, that the lightning sanctifies below
Whate'er it strikes;—yon head is doubly sacred now.[1]

XLII.[2]

Italia! O Italia! thou who hast   370
The fatal gift of beauty, which became
A funeral dower of present woes and past,
  On thy sweet brow is sorrow plowed by shame,
And annals graved in characters of flame.
O God! that thou wert in thy nakedness   375
Less lovely or more powerful, and couldst claim
Thy right, and awe the robbers back, who press
To shed thy blood, and drink the tears of thy distress;

XLIII.

Then mightst thou more appall; or, less desired,
Be homely and be peaceful, undeplored   380
For thy destructive charms; then, still untired,
  Would not be seen the armèd torrents poured
Down the deep Alps; nor would the hostile horde
Of many-nationed spoilers from the Po
Quaff blood and water; nor the stranger's sword   385
Be thy sad weapon of defense, and so,
Victor or vanquished, thou the slave of friend or foe.

XLIV.

Wandering in youth, I traced the path of him,[3]
The Roman friend of Rome's least mortal mind,

---

[1] " Before the remains of Ariosto were removed from the Benedictine church to the library of Ferrara, his bust, which surmounted the tomb, was struck by lightning, and a crown of iron laurels melted away " (BYRON).

[2] This stanza and the next, as Byron tells us in a note, are mainly a translation of a famous sonnet on Italy, by Filicaja, who died in 1707.

[3] Servius Sulpicius.

The friend of Tully :[1] as my bark did skim   390
The bright blue waters with a fanning wind,
Came Megara before me, and behind
Ægina lay, Piræus on the right,
And Corinth on the left; I lay reclined
Along the prow, and saw all these unite   395
In ruin, even as he had seen the desolate sight;

XLV.

For Time hath not rebuilt them, but upreared
Barbaric dwellings on their shattered site,
Which only make more mourned and more endeared
The few last rays of their far-scattered light,   400
And the crushed relics of their vanished might.
The Roman saw these tombs in his own age,
These sepulchers of cities, which excite
Sad wonder, and his yet surviving page
The moral lesson bears, drawn from such pilgrimage.   405

XLVI.

That page is now before me, and on mine
His country's ruin added to the mass
Of perished states he mourned in their decline,
And I in desolation: all that *was*
Of then destruction *is;* and now, alas!   410
Rome—Rome imperial, bows her to the storm,
In the same dust and blackness, and we pass
The skeleton of her Titanic form,
Wrecks of another world, whose ashes still are warm.

XLVII.

Yet, Italy! through every other land   415
Thy wrongs should ring, and shall, from side to side;

[1] Cicero.

Mother of Arts! as once of Arms; thy hand
Was then our guardian, and is still our guide;
Parent of our Religion![1] whom the wide
Nations have knelt to for the keys of heaven!   420
Europe, repentant of her parricide,
Shall yet redeem thee, and, all backward driven,
Roll the barbarian tide, and sue to be forgiven.[2]

XLVIII.

But Arno wins us to the fair white walls,
Where the Etrurian Athens claims and keeps   425
A softer feeling for her fairy halls.[3]
Girt by her theater of hills, she reaps
Her corn, and wine, and oil, and Plenty leaps
To laughing life, with her redundant horn.
Along the banks where smiling Arno sweeps   430
Was modern Luxury of Commerce born,
And buried Learning rose, redeemed to a new morn.

XLIX.

There, too, the goddess[4] loves in stone, and fills
The air around with beauty; we inhale
The ambrosial aspect, which, beheld, instills   435
Part of its immortality; the veil
Of heaven is half undrawn; within the pale
We stand, and in that form and face behold
What Mind can make, when Nature's self would fail;
And to the fond idolaters of old   440
Envy the innate flash which such a soul could mold:

[1] The original Christian church was fostered by Rome.
[2] What has been the progress of Italy since Byron lamented her decay?
[3] Florence is on the Arno.
[4] The Venus de Medici. Keene says: " It is now considered an uninspired copy by some trade artist living at Rome about the time of Augustus." Byron's taste was not always equal to his enthusiasm.

L.

We gaze and turn away, and know not where,
Dazzled and drunk with beauty, till the heart
Reels with its fullness; there—forever there—
Chained to the chariot of triumphal Art,   •   445
We stand as captives, and would not depart.
Away! —there need no words nor terms precise,
The paltry jargon of the marble mart,
Where Pedantry gulls Folly—we have eyes :[1]   449
Blood, pulse, and breast confirm the Dardan Shepherd's prize.[2]

LI.

Appearedst thou not to Paris in this guise?
Or to more deeply blest Anchises?[3] or,
In all thy perfect goddess-ship, when lies
Before thee thy own vanquished Lord of War ?[4]
And gazing in thy face as toward a star,   455
Laid on thy lap, his eyes to thee upturn,
Feeding on thy sweet cheek! while thy lips are
With lava kisses melting while they burn,
Showered on his eyelids, brow, and mouth, as from an urn?

LII.

Glowing, and circumfused in speechless love,   460
Their full divinity inadequate
That feeling to express, or to improve,
The gods become as mortals, and man's fate

---

[1] Does not even genius require education in order to judge correctly of
the fine arts, painting, sculpture, poetry? Byron remained in Florence only
a single day.   [2] Paris of Troy awarded the prize for beauty to Venus.
   [3] Anchises, the father of Æneas, was beloved by Venus.   [4] Mars.

Has moments like their brightest; but the weight
Of earth recoils upon us;—let it go!   465
We can recall such visions, and create,
From what has been, or might be, things which grow
Into thy statue's form, and look like gods below.

ι.

LIII.

I leave to learnèd fingers and wise hands,
The artist and his ape,[1] to teach and tell   470
How well his connoisseurship understands
The graceful bend, and the voluptuous swell:
Let these describe the undescribable:
I would not their vile breath should crisp the stream
Wherein that image shall forever dwell;   475
The unruffled mirror of the loveliest dream
That ever left the sky on the deep soul to beam.

LIV.

In Santa Croce's[2] holy precincts lie
Ashes which make it holier, dust which is
Even in itself an immortality,   480
Though there were nothing save the past, and this,
The particle of those sublimities
Which have relapsed to chaos: here repose
Angelo's,[3] Alfieri's[4] bones, and his,
The starry Galileo,[5] with his woes;   485
Here Machiavelli's[6] earth returned to whence it rose.

---

[1] Imitator.   [2] Holy Cross, a famous cathedral in Florence.
[3] Michael Angelo Buonarroti, the master painter, sculptor, and architect (born 1475, died 1564).   [4] Italian poet (born 1749, died 1803).
[5] Italian astronomer (born 1564, died 1642).
[6] Famous Italian political writer, author of The Prince (born 1469, died 1527).

LV.

These are four minds, which, like the elements,[1]
Might furnish forth creation : — Italy!
Time, which hath wronged thee with ten thousand rents
Of thine imperial garment, shall deny,　　　　　　490
And hath denied, to every other sky,
Spirits which soar from ruin : thy decay
Is still impregnate with divinity,
Which gilds it with revivifying ray;
Such as the great of yore, Canova[2] is to-day.　　495

LVI.

But where repose the all Etruscan three —
Dante, and Petrarch, and, scarce less than they,
The Bard of Prose,[3] creative spirit! he
Of the Hundred Tales of love — where did they lay
Their bones, distinguished from our common clay　　500
In death as life?　Are they resolved to dust,
And have their country's marbles naught to say?
Could not her quarries furnish forth one bust?
Did they not to her breast their filial earth intrust?

LVII.

Ungrateful Florence! Dante sleeps afar,[4]　　　.　　505
Like Scipio, buried by the upbraiding shore :
Thy factions,[5] in their worse than civil war,
Proscribed the bard whose name forevermore

---

[1] Earth, air, water, fire, or hot, cold, moist, dry.
[2] An Italian sculptor of Byron's day (born 1757, died 1822).
[3] Boccaccio, author of the Decameron, etc.　He was buried near Florence.
[4] In Ravenna.　　　　　　[5] Guelphs and Ghibellines,

Their children's children would in vain adore
With the remorse of ages; and the crown   510
Which Petrarch's laureate [1] brow supremely wore,
Upon a far and foreign soil had grown,
His life, his fame, his grave, though rifled—not thine own.

LVIII.

Boccaccio [2] to his parent earth bequeathed
His dust,—and lies it not her great among,   515
With many a sweet and solemn requiem breathed
O'er him who formed the Tuscan's siren tongue? [3]
That music in itself, whose sounds are song,
The poetry of speech?   No;—even his tomb
Uptorn, must bear the hyena bigot's wrong, [4]   520
No more amidst the meaner dead find room,
Nor claim a passing sigh, because it told for *whom!* [5]

LIX.

And Santa Croce [6] wants their mighty dust;
Yet for this want more noted, as of yore
The Cæsar's pageant, shorn of Brutus' bust,   525
Did but of Rome's best son remind her more: [7]
Happier Ravenna! on thy hoary shore,
Fortress of falling empire! honored sleeps

---

[1] Petrarch was crowned poet laureate at Rome in 1341.

[2] Boccaccio was buried near the place of his birth, Cetaldo.

[3] Boccaccio did for Italian prose what Wyclif did for English.   The Tuscan is the purest literary Italian.

[4] The hyena digs bodies from the grave.   Boccaccio's tombstone was torn away by bigot spite.

[5] "His tomb was not allowed to claim a passing sigh because its inscription mentioned the name of the person for whom the sigh was claimed, viz., Boccaccio, the enemy of the monks" (TOZER).

[6] Byron called Santa Croce the Westminster Abbey of Italy.

[7] Tacitus says the "bust was conspicuous by its absence."

The immortal exile;[1]—Arqua, too, her store
Of tuneful relics proudly claims and keeps,   530
While Florence vainly begs her banished dead and weeps.

LX.

What is her pyramid of precious stones?
Of porphyry, jasper, agate, and all hues
Of gem and marble, to incrust the bones
Of merchant dukes?[2] the momentary dews   535
Which, sparkling to the twilight stars, infuse
Freshness in the green turf that wraps the dead,
Whose names are mausoleums of the Muse,
Are gently pressed with far more reverent tread
Than ever paced the slab which paves the princely head. 540

LXI.

There be more things to greet the heart and eyes
In Arno's dome[3] of Art's most princely shrine,
Where Sculpture with her rainbow sister vies;
There be more marvels yet—but not for mine;
For I have been accustomed to entwine   545
My thoughts with Nature rather in the fields,
Than Art in galleries; though a work divine
Calls for my spirit's homage, yet it yields
Less than it feels, because the weapon which it wields

LXII.

Is of another temper, and I roam   550
By Thrasimene's lake,[4] in the defiles

[1] Dante, the greatest Italian poet.
[2] " I went to the Medici Chapel,—fine frippery, in great slabs of various
expensive stones, to commemorate fifty rotten and forgotten carcasses "
(BYRON).   [3] The Florence picture gallery.
[4] Near which the Roman army was defeated by Hannibal.

Fatal to Roman rashness, more at home;
For there the Carthaginian's warlike wiles
Come back before me, as his skill beguiles
The host between the mountains and the shore,   555
Where Courage falls in her despairing files,
And torrents, swoll'n to rivers with their gore,
Reek through the sultry plain, with legions scattered o'er,

LXIII.

Like to a forest felled by mountain winds;
And such the storm of battle on this day,   560
And such the frenzy, whose convulsion blinds
To all save carnage, that, beneath the fray,
An earthquake reeled unheededly away![1]
None felt stern Nature rocking at his feet,
And yawning forth a grave for those who lay   565
Upon their bucklers for a winding sheet;
Such is the absorbing hate when warring nations meet!

LXIV.

The Earth to them was as a rolling bark
Which bore them to Eternity; they saw
The Ocean round, but had no time to mark   570
The motions of their vessel; Nature's law,
In them suspended, recked not of the awe
Which reigns when mountains tremble, and the birds
Plunge in the clouds for refuge, and withdraw
From their down-toppling nests; and bellowing herds 575
Stumble o'er heaving plains, and man's dread hath no words.

LXV.

Far other scene is Thrasimene now;
Her lake a sheet of silver, and her plain

[1] An earthquake occurred while the battle was in progress.

Rent by no ravage save the gentle plow;
Her agèd trees rise thick as once the slain   580
Lay where their roots are; but a brook hath ta'en—
A little rill of scanty stream and bed—
A name of blood from that day's sanguine rain;
And Sanguinetto [1] tells ye where the dead
Made the earth wet, and turned the unwilling waters red. 585

LXVI.

But thou, Clitumnus! [2] in thy sweetest wave
Of the most living crystal that was e'er
The haunt of river nymph, to gaze and lave
Her limbs where nothing hid them, thou dost rear
Thy grassy banks whereon the milk-white steer   590
Grazes; [3] the purest god of gentle waters!
And most serene of aspect, and most clear;
Surely that stream was unprofaned by slaughters,
A mirror and a bath for Beauty's youngest daughters!

LXVII.

And on thy happy shore a Temple [4] still,   595
Of small and delicate proportion, keeps,
Upon a mild declivity of hill,
Its memory of thee; beneath it sweeps
Thy current's calmness; oft from out it leaps
The finny darter with the glittering scales,   600
Who dwells and revels in thy glassy deeps;
While, chance, some scattered water lily sails
Down where the shallower wave still tells its bubbling tales.

---

[1] The name of a brook; from *sanguis*, "blood."
[2] A small branch of the Tiber.
[3] " Unwatched, along Clitumnus
    Grazes the milk-white steer."
          MACAULAY'S *Lays of Ancient Rome.*
[4] A small chapel of white marble.

LXVIII.

Pass not unblessed the Genius of the place![1]
If through the air a zephyr more serene   605
Win to the brow, 'tis his; and if ye trace
Along his margin a more eloquent green,
If on the heart the freshness of the scene
Sprinkle its coolness, and from the dry dust
Of weary life a moment lave it clean   610
With Nature's baptism,—'tis to him ye must
Pay orisons[2] for this suspension of disgust.

LXIX.

The roar of waters!—from the headlong height
Velino cleaves the wave-worn precipice;
The fall of waters! rapid as the light   615
The flashing mass foams shaking the abyss;
The hell of waters! where they howl and hiss,
And boil in endless torture; while the sweat
Of their great agony, wrung out from this
Their Phlegethon,[3] curls round the rocks of jet   620
That guard the gulf around, in pitiless horror set,

LXX.

And mounts in spray the skies, and thence again
Returns in an unceasing shower, which round,
With its unemptied cloud of gentle rain,
Is an eternal April to the ground,   625
Making it all one emerald:—how profound
The gulf! and how the giant element
From rock to rock leaps with delirious bound,
Crushing the cliffs, which, downward worn and rent
With his fierce footsteps, yield in chasms a fearful vent!   630

---

[1] Pray to the local deity (*genius loci*).   [2] Prayers.   [3] A river in hell.

LXXI.

To the broad column which rolls on, and shows
More like the fountain of an infant sea
Torn from the womb of mountains by the throes
Of a new world, than only thus to be
Parent of rivers, which flow gushingly,   635
With many windings, through the vale:—Look back!
Lo! where it comes like an eternity,
As if to sweep down all things in its track,
Charming the eye with dread,—a matchless cataract,

LXXII.

Horribly beautiful! but on the verge,   640
From side to side, beneath the glittering morn,
An Iris sits, amidst the infernal surge,
Like Hope upon a deathbed, and, unworn
Its steady dyes, while all around is torn
By the distracted waters, bears serene   645
Its brilliant hues with all their beams unshorn:
Resembling, 'mid the torture of the scene,
Love watching Madness with unalterable mien.[1]

LXXIII.

Once more upon the woody Apennine,
The infant Alps, which—had I not before   650
Gazed on their mightier parents, where the pine
Sits on more shaggy summits, and where roar
The thundering lauwine [2]—might be worshiped more;
But I have seen the soaring Jungfrau rear

[1] The description of the waterfall of Terni, on the Velino River, deserves a very careful reading.

[2] " Byron did not know German.   Had he done so he would not have used *Lauwine*, or *Lawine*, the ordinary German word for ' an avalanche,' as plural " (TOZER).

Her never-trodden [1] snow, and seen the hoar   655
Glaciers of bleak Mont Blanc both far and near,
And in Chimari heard the thunder hills of fear,

LXXIV.

Th' Acroceraunian mountains of old name;
And on Parnassus seen the eagles fly
Like spirits of the spot, as 'twere for fame,   660
For still they soared unutterably high:
I've looked on Ida with a Trojan's eye; [2]
Athos, Olympus, Ætna, Atlas, made
These hills seem things of lesser dignity,
All, save the lone Soracte's height, displayed   665
Not *now* [3] in snow, which asks the lyric Roman's aid

LXXV.

For our remembrance, and from out the plain
Heaves like a long-swept wave about to break,
And on the curl hangs pausing: not in vain
May he, who will, his recollections rake,   670
And quote in classic raptures, and awake
The hills with Latian echoes; I abhorred [4]
Too much, to conquer for the poet's sake,
The drilled dull lesson, forced down word by word
In my repugnant youth, with pleasure to record   675

LXXVI.

Aught that recalls the daily drug which turned
My sickening memory; and, though Time hath taught

---

[1] The Jungfrau has often been climbed.
[2] Mount Ida is above Troy.
[3] Horace mentions snow on Mount Soracte, a high hill near Rome.
[4] This should interest teachers and students of poetry, especially of classic

My mind to meditate what then it learned,
Yet such the fixed inveteracy wrought
By the impatience of my early thought,   680
That, with the freshness wearing out before
My mind could relish what it might have sought,
If free to choose, I cannot now restore
Its health; but what it then detested, still abhor.

LXXVII.

Then farewell, Horace; whom I hated so,   685
Not for thy faults, but mine; it is a curse
To understand, not feel thy lyric flow,
To comprehend, but never love thy verse:
Although no deeper Moralist rehearse
Our little life, nor Bard prescribe his art,   690
Nor livelier Satirist the conscience pierce,
Awakening without wounding the touched heart,
Yet fare thee well—upon Soracte's ridge we part.

LXXVIII.

O Rome! my country! city of the soul!
The orphans of the heart must turn to thee,   695
Lone mother of dead empires! and control
In their shut breasts their petty misery.

verse.   Mr. Rolfe says: "It is remarkable that this passage has not been
quoted in the recent attacks upon the study of Latin and Greek in our schools.
It might well be used in the criticism of the methods of study." Byron
himself said: "I wish to express that we become tired of the task before we
can comprehend the beauty; that we learn by rote before we can get by heart;
that the freshness is worn away, and the future pleasure and advantage dead-
ened and destroyed, by the didactic anticipation at an age when we can neither
feel nor understand the power of compositions which it requires an acquaint-
ance with life, as well as Latin and Greek, to relish or to reason upon.   For
the same reason we never can be aware of the fullness of some of the finest
passages of Shakespeare."

8

What are our woes and sufferance?   Come and see
The cypress, hear the owl, and plod your way
O'er steps of broken thrones and temples, Ye!   700
Whose agonies are evils of a day—
A world is at our feet as fragile as our clay.

LXXIX.

The Niobe[1] of nations! there she stands,
Childless and crownless, in her voiceless woe;
An empty urn within her withered hands,   705
Whose holy dust was scattered long ago;
The Scipios' tomb contains no ashes now;
The very sepulchers lie tenantless
Of their heroic dwellers: dost thou flow,
Old Tiber! through a marble wilderness?   710
Rise, with thy yellow waves, and mantle her distress.

LXXX.

The Goth, the Christian, Time, War, Flood, and Fire,
Have dealt upon the seven-hilled city's pride;[2]
She saw her glories star by star expire,
And up the steep barbarian monarchs ride,   715
Where the car climbed the Capitol; far and wide
Temple and tower went down, nor left a site:
Chaos of ruins! who shall trace the void,
O'er the dim fragments cast a lunar light,
And say, "here was, or is," where all is doubly night?   720

LXXXI.

The double night of ages, and of her,
Night's daughter, Ignorance, hath wrapt and wrap

[1] The Greek goddess who mourned her twelve children, slain by Apollo and Artemis. (See mythology for this and many other classic allusions.)

[2] With the aid of some text-book on history, recount briefly the great events suggested in this and other following stanzas.

All round us: we but feel our way to err:
The ocean hath its chart, the stars their map,
And Knowledge spreads them on her ample lap;   725
But Rome is as the desert, where we steer
Stumbling o'er recollections; now we clap
Our hands, and cry " Eureka!" it is clear—
When but some false mirage of ruin rises near.

LXXXII.

Alas! the lofty city! and alas!   730
The trebly hundred triumphs![1] and the day
When Brutus made the dagger's edge surpass
The conqueror's sword in bearing fame away![2]
Alas, for Tully's[3] voice, and Vergil's lay,
And Livy's pictured page!—but these shall be   735
Her resurrection; all beside—decay.
Alas, for Earth, for never shall we see,
That brightness in her eye she bore when Rome was free!

LXXXIII.

O thou, whose chariot rolled on Fortune's wheel,
Triumphant Sylla![4]   Thou, who didst subdue   740
Thy country's foes ere thou wouldst pause to feel
The wrath of thy own wrongs, or reap the due
Of hoarded vengeance till thine eagles flew
O'er prostrate Asia;—thou, who with thy frown
Annihilated senates—Roman, too,   745
With all thy vices, for thou didst lay down
With an atoning smile a more than earthly crown—

[1] " Orosius gives three hundred and twenty for the number of triumphs "
(BYRON).
[2] The killing of Cæsar.   [3] Cicero.
[4] Lucius Cornelius Sulla, Roman statesman and general, who conquered
Asia Minor.

LXXXIV.

The dictatorial wreath [1]—couldst thou divine
To what would one day dwindle that which made
Thee more than mortal? and that so supine   750
By aught than Romans Rome should thus be laid?
She who was named Eternal, and arrayed
Her warriors but to conquer—she who veiled
Earth with her haughty shadow, and displayed,
Until the o'er-canopied horizon failed,   755
Her rushing wings—Oh! she who was Almighty hailed!

LXXXV.

Sylla was first of victors; but our own,
The sagest of usurpers, Cromwell! —he
Too swept off senates while he hewed the throne
Down to a block—immortal rebel!   See   760
What crimes it costs to be a moment free,
And famous through all ages! but beneath
His fate the moral lurks of destiny;
His day of double victory and death [2]   764
Beheld him win two realms, and, happier, yield his breath.[3]

LXXXVI.

[1]

The third of the same moon whose former course
Had all but crowned him, on the selfsame day
Deposed him gently from his throne of force,
And laid him with the earth's preceding clay.

[1] Sulla was made dictator B.C. 81, but resigned his great office B.C. 79.

[2] Cromwell won the battle of Dunbar, September 3, 1650, that of Worcester, September 3, 1651, and died September 3, 1658.

[3] This graphic summary of Cromwell's character and career is interesting; is it just?   Was Cromwell cruel?   (See Carlyle's Letters and Speeches of Cromwell.)

And showed not Fortune thus how fame and sway,   770
And all we deem delightful, and consume
Our souls to compass through each arduous way,
Are in her eyes less happy than the tomb?
Were they but so in man's, how different were his doom!

LXXXVII.

And thou, dread statue![1] yet existent in   775
The austerest form of naked majesty,
Thou who beheldest, 'mid the assassins' din,
At thy bathed base the bloody Cæsar lie,
Folding his robe in dying dignity,
An offering to thine altar from the queen   780
Of gods and men, great Nemesis![2] did he die,
And thou, too, perish, Pompey? have ye been
Victors of countless kings, or puppets of a scene?

LXXXVIII.

And thou, the thunder-stricken nurse of Rome!
She wolf![3] whose brazen-imaged dugs impart   785
The milk of conquest yet within the dome
Where, as a monument of antique art,
Thou standest:—Mother of the mighty heart,
Which the great founder sucked from thy wild teat,
Scorched by the Roman Jove's ethereal dart,   790
And thy limbs black with lightning—dost thou yet
Guard thine immortal cubs, nor thy fond charge forget?

---

[1] The statue of Pompey in the Spada Palace at Rome.

> " And in his mantle muffling up his face,
>   Even at the base of Pompey's statua,
>   Which all the while ran blood, great Cæsar fell."
>   SHAKESPEARE'S *Julius Cæsar*, iii. 2.

[2] The goddess of retribution.
[3] The bronze wolf, supposed to have been struck by lightning.

LXXXIX.

Thou dost; but all thy foster babes are dead—
The men of iron: and the world hath reared
Cities from out their sepulchers: men bled   795
In imitation of the things they feared,
And fought and conquered, and the same course steered,
At apish distance; but as yet none have,
Nor could, the same supremacy have neared,
Save one vain man,[1] who is not in the grave,   800
But, vanquished by himself, to his own slaves a slave—

XC.

The fool of false dominion—and a kind
Of bastard Cæsar, following him of old
With steps unequal; for the Roman's mind
Was modeled in a less terrestrial mold,   805
With passions fiercer, yet a judgment cold,
And an immortal instinct which redeemed
The frailties of a heart so soft, yet bold.
Alcides[2] with the distaff now he seemed
At Cleopatra's feet,—and now himself he beamed,   810

XCI.

And came—and saw—and conquered!   But the man[3]
Who would have tamed his eagles down to flee,
Like a trained falcon, in the Gallic[4] van,
Which he, in sooth, long led to victory,
With a deaf heart which never seemed to be   815
A listener to itself, was strangely framed;

---

[1] Napoleon.   [2] Hercules held a distaff for Omphale, queen of Lydia.
[3] Napoleon.   [4] French.

With but one weakest weakness—vanity:
Coquettish in ambition, still he aimed—
At what? can he avouch, or answer what he claimed?

XCII.

And would be all or nothing—nor could wait   820
For the sure grave to level him; few years
Had fixed him with the Cæsars in his fate,
On whom we tread: For *this* the conqueror rears
The arch of triumph! and for this the tears
And blood of earth flow on as they have flowed,   825
An universal deluge, which appears
Without an ark for wretched man's abode,
And ebbs but to reflow!   Renew thy rainbow, God![1]

XCIII.[2]

What from this barren being do we reap?
Our senses narrow, and our reason frail,   830
Life short, and truth a gem which loves the deep,
And all things weighed in custom's falsest scale;
Opinion an omnipotence,—whose veil
Mantles the earth with darkness, until right
And wrong are accidents, and men grow pale   835
Lest their own judgments should become too bright,
And their free thoughts be crimes, and earth have too much
        light.

XCIV.

And thus they plod in sluggish misery,
Rotting from sire to son, and age to age,

---

[1] Gen. ix. 13.   Byron makes beautiful poetical use of the Scripture allusion here.
[2] Mark the fervid protest against oppression and wrong in Stanzas XCIII. and XCIV.   Byron's was always a voice for liberty.

Proud of their trampled nature, and so die,   840
Bequeathing their hereditary rage
To the new race of inborn slaves, who wage
War for their chains, and rather than be free,
Bleed gladiator-like, and still engage
Within the same arena where they see   845
Their fellows fall before, like leaves of the same tree.

XCV.

I speak not of men's creeds—they rest between
Man and his Maker—but of things allowed,
Averred, and known, and daily, hourly seen—
The yoke that is upon us doubly bowed,   ,   850
And the intent of tyranny avowed,
The edict of Earth's rulers, who are grown
The apes of him who humbled once the proud,
And shook them from their slumbers on the throne:
Too glorious, were this all his mighty arm had done.   855

XCVI.

Can tyrants but by tyrants conquered be,
And Freedom find no champion and no child
Such as Columbia[1] saw arise when she
Sprung forth a Pallas, armed and undefiled?
Or must such minds be nourished in the wild,   860
Deep in the unpruned forest, 'midst the roar
Of cataracts, where nursing Nature smiled
On infant Washington?   Has Earth no more
Such seeds within her breast, or Europe no such shore?

XCVII.

But France got drunk with blood to vomit crime,[2]   865
And fatal have her Saturnalia been

---

[1] American students need no note to interpret this.
[2] " A coarse but powerful image " (KEENE).

To Freedom's cause, in every age and clime;
Because the deadly days which we have seen,
And vile Ambition, that built up between
Man and his hopes an adamantine wall,   870
And the base pageant last upon the scene,
Are grown the pretext for the eternal thrall
Which nips life's tree, and dooms man's worst—his second fall.

XCVIII.[1]

Yet, Freedom! yet thy banner, torn, but flying,
Streams like the thunderstorm *against* the wind; 875
Thy trumpet voice, though broken now and dying,
The loudest still the tempest leaves behind;
Thy tree hath lost its blossoms, and the rind,
Chopped by the ax, looks rough and little worth,
But the sap lasts,—and still the seed we find   880
Sown deep, even in the bosom of the North;
So shall a better spring less bitter fruit bring forth.

XCIX.[2]

There is a stern round tower of other days,
Firm as a fortress, with its fence of stone,
Such as an army's baffled strength delays,   885
Standing with half its battlements alone,
And with two thousand years of ivy grown,
The garland of eternity, where wave
 The green leaves over all by time o'erthrown;—
What was this tower of strength? within its cave 890
What treasure lay so locked, so hid?—A woman's grave.

---

1 A splendid stanza,—strong, true, and soul-stirring. Study its several bold metaphors, especially the first one.

2 Here we have another of Byron's abrupt changes of theme. The six following stanzas are reflections on the tomb of Cæcilia Metella, daughter of Metellus Creticus, and wife of M. Crassus.

C.

But who was she, the lady of the dead,
Tombed in a palace?   Was she chaste and fair?
Worthy a king's, or more—a Roman's bed?
What race of chiefs and heroes did she bear?   895
What daughter of her beauties was the heir?
How lived, how loved, how died she?   Was she not
So honored—and conspicuously there,
Where meaner relics must not dare to rot,
Placed to commemorate a more than mortal lot?   900

CI.

Was she as those who love their lords, or they
Who love the lords of others? such have been
Even in the olden time, Rome's annals say.
Was she a matron of Cornelia's mien,
Or the light air of Egypt's graceful queen,   905
Profuse of joy—or 'gainst it did she war
Inveterate in virtue?   Did she lean
To the soft side of the heart, or wisely bar
Love from amongst her griefs?—for such the affections are.

CII.

Perchance she died in youth: it may be, bowed   910
With woes far heavier than the ponderous tomb
That weighed upon her gentle dust, a cloud
Might gather o'er her beauty, and a gloom
In her dark eye, prophetic of the doom
Heaven gives its favorites—early death; yet shed   915
A sunset charm around her, and illume
With hectic light, the Hesperus [1] of the dead,
Of her consuming cheek the autumnal leaflike red.

[1] Evening star,

CIII.

Perchance she died in age—surviving all,
Charms, kindred, children—with the silver gray   920
On her long tresses, which might yet recall,
It may be, still a something of the day
When they were braided, and her proud array
And lovely form were envied, praised, and eyed
By Rome—But whither would Conjecture stray?   925
Thus much alone we know—Metella died,
The wealthiest Roman's [1] wife: Behold his love or pride!

CIV.

I know not why—but standing thus by thee
It seems as if I had thine inmate known,
Thou tomb! and other days come back on me   930
With recollected music, though the tone
Is changed and solemn, like the cloudy groan
Of dying thunder on the distant wind;
Yet could I seat me by this ivied stone
Till I had bodied forth the heated mind   935
Forms from the floating wreck which Ruin leaves behind;

CV.[2]

And from the planks, far shattered o'er the rocks,
Built me a little bark of hope, once more
To battle with the ocean and the shocks
Of the loud breakers, and the ceaseless roar   940
Which rushes on the solitary shore
Where all lies foundered that was ever dear:

[1] " Crassus, whose agnomen was Dives " (TOZER).
[2] There is in this stanza a sweet sadness characteristic of Byron's gentlest
mood.

But could I gather from the wave-worn store
  Enough for my rude boat, where should I steer?   944
There wooes no home, nor hope, nor life, save what is here.

CVI.

Then let the winds howl on![1] their harmony
  Shall henceforth be my music, and the night
The sound shall temper with the owlets' cry,
  As I now hear them, in the fading light
Dim o'er the bird of darkness' native site,   950
  Answering each other on the Palatine,[2]
With their large eyes, all glistening gray and bright,
  And sailing pinions.—Upon such a shrine
What are our petty griefs?—let me not number mine.

CVII.

Cypress and ivy, weed and wallflower grown   955
  Matted and massed together, hillocks heaped
On what were chambers, arch crushed, column strown
  In fragments, choked-up vaults, and frescoes steeped
In subterranean damps, where the owl peeped,
  Deeming it midnight:—Temples, baths, or halls?   960
Pronounce who can; for all that Learning reaped
  From her research hath been, that these are walls—
Behold the Imperial Mount![3] 'tis thus the mighty falls.

CVIII.

There is the moral of all human tales;
  'Tis but the same rehearsal of the past,   965

---

[1] The passage beginning, "Then let the winds," and ending, "burns with Cicero," Stanzas CVI.–CXII., is one of Byron's noblest, and one of the finest in English poetry.   [2] One of Rome's seven hills.

[3] Augustus Cæsar had his palace on this mount.

First Freedom, and then Glory—when that fails,
Wealth, vice, corruption,—barbarism at last.
And History, with all her volumes vast,
Hath but *one* page,—'tis better written here
Where gorgeous Tyranny hath thus amassed   970
All treasures, all delights, that eye or ear,
Heart, soul could seek, tongue ask—Away with words! draw
     near,

CIX.

Admire, exult, despise, laugh, weep,—for here
There is such matter for all feeling:—Man!
Thou pendulum betwixt a smile and tear,[1]   975
Ages and realms are crowded in this span,
This mountain, whose obliterated plan
The pyramid of empires pinnacled,
Of Glory's gewgaws[2] shining in the van
Till the sun's rays with added flame were filled!   980
Where are its golden roofs? where those who dared to build?

CX.

Tully was not so eloquent as thou,
Thou nameless column[3] with the buried base!
What are the laurels of the Cæsar's brow?
Crown me with ivy from his dwelling place.[4]   985
Whose arch or pillar meets me in the face,
Titus' or Trajan's?   No—'tis that of Time:
Triumph, arch, pillar, all he doth displace
Scoffing; and apostolic statues climb
To crush the imperial urn,[5] whose ashes slept sublime, 990

[1] A famous line.   [2] Happy alliteration.
[3] Now discovered to have been erected to Phocus, an emperor.
[4] A suggestive and beautiful line.
[5] The urn of Trajan was replaced by a statue of St. Peter.

CXI.

Buried in air, the deep-blue sky of Rome,
And looking to the stars: they had contained
A spirit which with these would find a home,
The last of those who o'er the whole earth reigned,
The Roman globe, for after none sustained,   995
But yielded back his conquests:—he was more
Than a mere Alexander, and, unstained
With household blood and wine, serenely wore
His sovereign virtues—still we Trajan's name adore.

CXII.

Where is the rock of Triumph,[1] the high place   1000
Where Rome embraced her heroes? where the steep
Tarpeian? fittest goal of Treason's race,
The promontory whence the Traitor's Leap
Cured all ambition.   Did the conquerors heap
Their spoils here?   Yes; and in yon field below,   1005
A thousand years of silenced factions sleep—
The forum, where the immortal accents glow,
And still the eloquent air breathes—burns[2] with Cicero!

CXIII.

The field of freedom, faction, fame, and blood:
Here a proud people's passions were exhaled,   1010
From the first hour of empire in the bud
To that when further worlds to conquer failed;

[1] The Tarpeian Rock.   What says Roman history of it?
[2] " Thoughts that breathe, and words that burn " (GRAY's Progress of Poesy, line 110).

But long before had Freedom's face been veiled,
And Anarchy assumed her attributes;
Till every lawless soldier who assailed   1015
Trod on the trembling senate's slavish mutes,
Or raised the venal voice of baser prostitutes.[1]

CXIV.

Then turn we to her latest tribune's name,
From her ten thousand tyrants turn to thee,
Redeemer of dark centuries of shame—   1020
The friend of Petrarch—hope of Italy—
Rienzi![2] last of Romans!   While the tree
Of freedom's withered trunk puts forth a leaf,
Even for thy tomb a garland let it be—
The forum's champion, and the people's chief—   1025
Her new-born Numa[3] thou—with reign, alas! too brief.

CXV.

Egeria! sweet creation of some heart
Which found no mortal resting place so fair
As thine ideal breast; whate'er thou art
Or wert,—a young Aurora of the air,   1030
The nympholepsy[4] of some fond despair;
Or, it might be, a beauty of the earth,
Who found a more than common votary there
Too much adoring; whatsoe'er thy birth,
Thou wert a beautiful thought, and softly bodied forth.   1035

---

1 This stanza briefly describes the decline of the Roman empire.
2 Every schoolboy knows Miss Mitford's "I come not here to talk."
Read Gibbon's entertaining chapter on Rienzi.
3 Rome's (legendary) second king. He is fabled to have wedded the
nymph Egeria. Much poetry has been written about Egeria.
4 " An ecstasy; a divine frenzy " (Century Dictionary).

CXVI.

The mosses of thy fountain [1] still are sprinkled
With thine Elysian waterdrops; the face
Of thy cave-guarded spring, with years unwrinkled,
Reflects the meek-eyed genius of the place,
Whose green, wild margin now no more erase   1040
Art's works; nor must the delicate waters sleep,
Prisoned in marble, bubbling from the base
Of the cleft statue,[2] with a gentle leap
The rill runs o'er, and round fern, flowers, and ivy creep,

CXVII.

Fantastically tangled: the green hills   1045
Are clothed with early blossoms, through the grass
The quick-eyed lizard rustles, and the bills
Of summer birds sing welcome as ye pass;
Flowers fresh in hue, and many in their class,
Implore the pausing step, and with their dyes   1050
Dance in the soft breeze in a fairy mass;
The sweetness of the violet's deep-blue eyes,
Kissed by the breath of heaven, seems colored by its skies.

CXVIII.

Here didst thou dwell, in this enchanted cover,
Egeria! thy all-heavenly bosom beating   1055
For the far footsteps of thy mortal lover;
The purple Midnight [3] veiled that mystic meeting

[1] The " grotto of Egeria " is near Rome.
[2] A broken statue near the fountain.
[3] " Allusion to the warm darkness of southern night, so different from the steely blue of high latitudes " (KEENE).

With her most starry canopy, and seating
Thyself by thine adorer, what befell ?
This cave was surely shaped out for the greeting   1060
Of an enamored goddess, and the cell
Haunted by holy Love—the earliest oracle!

CXIX.

And didst thou not, thy breast to his replying,
Blend a celestial with a human heart ;
And Love, which dies as it was born, in sighing,   1065
Share with immortal transports? could thine art
Make them indeed immortal, and impart
The purity of heaven to earthly joys,
Expel the venom and not blunt the dart—
The dull satiety which all destroys—   1070
And root from out the soul the deadly weed which cloys?

CXX.

Alas! our young affections run to waste,
Or water but the desert ; whence arise
But weeds of dark luxuriance, tares of haste,
Rank at the core, though tempting to the eyes,   1075
Flowers whose wild odors breathe but agonies,
And trees whose gums are poison ; such the plants
Which spring beneath her steps as Passion flies
O'er the world's wilderness, and vainly pants
For some celestial fruit forbidden to our wants.   1080

CXXI.

O Love! no habitant of earth thou art—
An unseen seraph, we believe in thee,—
A faith whose martyrs are the broken heart,—
But never yet hath seen, nor e'er shall see

9

The naked eye, thy form, as it should be;   1085
The mind hath made thee, as it peopled heaven,
Even with its own desiring fantasy,
And to a thought such shape and image given,
As haunts the unquenched soul—parched, wearied, wrung,
        and riven.

CXXII.

Of its own beauty is the mind diseased,   1090
And fevers into false creation : — where,
Where are the forms the sculptor's soul hath seized?
In him alone.   Can Nature show so fair?
Where are the charms and virtues which we dare
Conceive in boyhood and pursue as men,   1095
The unreached Paradise of our despair,
Which o'er-informs the pencil and the pen,
And overpowers the page where it would bloom again?

CXXIII.

Who loves, raves—'tis youth's frenzy—but the cure
Is bitterer still, as charm by charm unwinds   1100
Which robed our idols, and we see too sure
Nor worth nor beauty dwells from out the mind's
Ideal shape of such; yet still it binds
The fatal spell, and still it draws us on,
Reaping the whirlwind from the oft-sown winds;[1]   1105
The stubborn heart, its alchemy [2] begun,
Seems ever near the prize—wealthiest when most undone.

CXXIV.[3]

We wither from our youth, we gasp away—
Sick—sick; unfound the boon, unslaked the thirst,

---

[1] Hosea viii. 7.   [2] Changing base metals into gold.
[3] Fine poetry, but morose thought.

Though to the last, in verge of our decay,   1110
Some phantom lures, such as we sought at first—
But all too late,—so are we doubly cursed.
Love, fame, ambition, avarice—'tis the same,
Each idle, and all ill, and none the worst—
For all are meteors with a different name,   1115
And Death the sable smoke where vanishes the flame.

CXXV.[1]

Few—none—find what they love or could have loved,
Though accident, blind contact, and the strong
Necessity of loving, have removed
Antipathies—but to recur, ere long,   1120
Envenomed with irrevocable wrong;
And Circumstance, that unspiritual god
And miscreator, makes and helps along
Our coming evils with a crutchlike rod,   1124
Whose touch turns Hope to dust,—the dust we all have trod.

CXXVI.

Our life is a false nature : 'tis not in
The harmony of things,—this hard decree,
This uneradicable taint of sin,
This boundless upas, this all-blasting tree,
Whose root is earth, whose leaves and branches be   1130
The skies which rain their plagues on men like dew—
Disease, death, bondage—all the woes we see,
And worse, the woes we see not—which throb through
The immedicable soul, with heartaches ever new.

CXXVII.

Yet let us ponder boldly—'tis a base   1135
Abandonment of reason to resign

1 This is a personal wail.

Our right of thought—our last and only place
Of refuge; this, at least, shall still be mine:
Though from our birth the faculty divine
Is chained and tortured—cabined, cribbed, confined,[1] 1140
And bred in darkness, lest the truth should shine
Too brightly on the unpreparèd mind,
The beam pours in, for time and skill will couch [2] the blind.

CXXVIII.[3]

Arches on arches! as it were that Rome,
Collecting the chief trophies of her line,   1145
Would build up all her triumphs in one dome,
Her Coliseum stands; the moonbeams shine
As 'twere its natural torches, for divine
Should be the light which streams here to illume
This long-explored but still exhaustless mine   1150
Of contemplation; and the azure gloom
Of an Italian night, where the deep skies assume

CXXIX.

Hues which have words, and speak to ye of heaven,
Floats o'er this vast and wondrous monument,
And shadows forth its glory.   There is given   1155
Unto the things of earth, which Time hath bent,
A spirit's feeling, and where he hath leant
His hand, but broke his scythe, there is a power
And magic in the ruined battlement,
For which the palace of the present hour   1160
Must yield its pomp, and wait till ages are its dower.

---

[1] Cf. Macbeth, iii. iv.

[2] " Couch " here means to remove a cataract from the eye.

[3] Byron's melancholy musings now seek solace in contemplating the ruins of the Coliseum.

CXXX.

O Time! the beautifier of the dead,
Adorner of the ruin, comforter
And only healer when the heart hath bled;
Time! the corrector where our judgments err,   1165
The test of truth, love—sole philosopher,
For all beside are sophists—from thy thrift,
Which never loses though it doth defer—
Time, the avenger! unto thee I lift
My hands, and eyes, and heart, and crave of thee a gift: 1170

CXXXI.

Amidst this wreck, where thou hast made a shrine
And temple more divinely desolate,
Among thy mightier offerings here are mine,
Ruins of years, though few, yet full of fate:
If thou hast ever seen me too elate,   1175
Hear me not; but if calmly I have borne
Good, and reserved my pride against the hate
Which shall not whelm me, let me not have worn
This iron in my soul in vain—shall *they* not mourn? [1]

CXXXII.

And thou, who never yet of human wrong   1180
Left the unbalanced scale, great Nemesis!
Here, where the ancient paid thee homage long—
Thou who didst call the Furies from the abyss,
And round Orestes [2] bade them howl and hiss
For that unnatural retribution—just,   1185

[1] Is not this vindictive?
[2] Orestes was pursued by the Furies for having slain his mother.

Had it but been from hands less near—in this
Thy former realm, I call thee from the dust!
Dost thou not hear my heart?—Awake! thou shalt, and must.

CXXXIII.

It is not that I may not have incurred
For my ancestral faults or mine the wound　　　　1190
I bleed withal, and, had it been conferred
With a just weapon, it had flowed unbound;
But now my blood shall not sink in the ground;
To thee I do devote it—*thou* shalt take
The vengeance, which shall yet be sought and found, 1195
Which if *I* have not taken for the sake—
But let that pass—I sleep, but thou shalt yet awake.

CXXXIV.

And if my voice break forth, 'tis not that now
I shrink from what is suffered: let him speak
Who hath beheld decline upon my brow,　　　　1200
Or seen my mind's convulsion leave it weak;
But in this page a record will I seek.
Not in the air shall these my words disperse,
Though I be ashes; a far hour shall wreak
The deep prophetic fullness of this verse,　　　　1205
And pile on human heads the mountain of my curse!

CXXXV.

That curse shall be Forgiveness.[1]—Have I not—
Hear me, my mother Earth! behold it, Heaven!—
Have I not had to wrestle with my lot?
Have I not suffered things to be forgiven?　　　　1210

---

[1] A critic aptly calls this passage a " boisterous pardon."

Have I not had my brain seared, my heart riven,
Hopes sapped, name blighted, Life's life lied away?
And only not to desperation driven,
Because not altogether of such clay
As rots into the souls of those whom I survey.   1215

CXXXVI.

From mighty wrongs to petty perfidy
Have I not seen what human things could do?
From the loud roar of foaming calumny [1]
To the small whisper of the as paltry few,
And subtler venom of the reptile crew,   1220
The Janus [2] glance of whose significant eye,
Learning to lie with silence, would *seem* true,
And without utterance, save the shrug or sigh,
Deal round to happy fools its speechless obloquy.

CXXXVII.

But I have lived, and have not lived in vain: 1225
My mind may lose its force, my blood its fire,
And my frame perish even in conquering pain;
But there is that within me which shall tire
Torture and Time, and breathe when I expire;
Something unearthly, which they deem not of,   1230
Like the remembered tone of a mute lyre,
Shall on their softened spirits sink, and move
In hearts all rocky now the late remorse of love.

CXXXVIII.

The seal is set.[3]—Now welcome, thou dread power!
Nameless, yet thus omnipotent, which here   1235

---

[1] A felicitous line.   [2] The two-faced god.
[3] Keene quotes Sir Walter Scott's "A minstrel's malison is set."

Walk'st in the shadow of the midnight hour
With a deep awe, yet all distinct from fear;
Thy haunts are ever where the dead walls rear
Their ivy mantles, and the solemn scene
Derives from thee a sense so deep and clear   1240
That we become a part of what has been,
And grow unto the spot, all-seeing but unseen.

CXXXIX.

And here the buzz of eager nations ran,
In murmured pity, or loud-roared applause,
As man was slaughtered by his fellow-man.   1245
And wherefore slaughtered? wherefore, but because
Such were the bloody Circus' genial laws,
And the imperial pleasure.—Wherefore not?
What matters where we fall to fill the maws [1]
Of worms—on battle plains or listed spot?   1250
Both are but theaters where the chief actors rot.

CXL.

I see before me the Gladiator lie: [2]
He leans upon his hand—his manly brow
Consents to death, but conquers agony,
And his drooped head sinks gradually low—   1255
And through his side the last drops, ebbing slow
From the red gash, fall heavy, one by one,
Like the first of a thundershower; and now
The arena swims around him—he is gone,
Ere ceased the inhuman shout which hailed the wretch who
          won.   1260

[1] " Our monuments shall be the maws of kites " (Macbeth, iii. iv.).
[2] Copies in plaster of The Dying Gladiator, a statue in the museum at
Rome, may be seen in most art galleries.

CXLI.

He heard it, but he heeded not—his eyes
Were with his heart, and that was far away;
He recked not of the life he lost nor prize,
But where his rude hut by the Danube lay,
There were his young barbarians all at play,   1265
There was their Dacian mother—he, their sire,
Butchered to make a Roman holiday—
All this rushed with his blood—Shall he expire,
And unavenged?   Arise! ye Goths,[1] and glut your ire

CXLII.

But here, where Murder breathed her bloody steam;   1270
And here, where buzzing nations choked the ways,
And roared or murmured like a mountain stream
Dashing or winding as its torrent strays;
Here, where the Roman million's blame or praise
Was death or life, the playthings of a crowd,   1275
My voice sounds much [2]—and fall the stars' faint rays
On the arena void—seats crushed—walls bowed—
And galleries, where my steps seem echoes strangely loud.

CXLIII.

A ruin—yet what ruin! from its mass
Walls, palaces, half cities, have been reared;[3]   1280
Yet oft the enormous skeleton ye pass,
And marvel where the spoil could have appeared.
Hath it indeed been plundered, or but cleared?
Alas! developed, opens the decay,

---

1 *Did* the Goths rise and glut their ire?
2 I.e., in the silence of the solitary place.
3 Read what Gibbon and others have written on the Coliseum.

When the colossal fabric's form is neared :   1285
It will not bear the brightness of the day,
Which streams too much on all years, man, have reft away.

CXLIV.

But when the rising moon begins to climb
Its topmost arch, and gently pauses there ;
When the stars twinkle through the loops of time,   1290
And the low night breeze waves along the air
The garland forest, which the gray walls wear,
Like laurels on the bald first Cæsar's head ;
When the light shines serene, but doth not glare,
Then in this magic circle raise the dead :   1295
Heroes have trod this spot—'tis on their dust ye tread.

CXLV.

" While stands the Coliseum, Rome shall stand ;
When falls the Coliseum, Rome shall fall ;
And when Rome falls—the World." [1] From our own land
Thus spake the pilgrims o'er this mighty wall   1300
In Saxon times, which we are wont to call
Ancient ; and these three mortal things are still
On their foundations, and unaltered all ;
Rome and her Ruin past Redemption's skill,   1304
The World, the same wide den—of thieves, or what ye will.

CXLVI.

Simple, erect, severe, austere, sublime [2]—
Shrine of all saints and temple of all gods,

---

[1] " This is quoted in the Decline and Fall of the Roman Empire as a proof that the Coliseum was entire when seen by the Anglo-Saxon pilgrims at the end of the seventh or the beginning of the eighth century " (BYRON).

[2] The Pantheon was built B.C. 27.

From Jove to Jesus—spared and blest by time;
Looking tranquillity, while falls or nods
Arch, empire, each thing round thee, and man plods   1310
His way through thorns to ashes—glorious dome!
Shalt thou not last?   Time's scythe and tyrants' rods
Shiver upon thee—sanctuary and home
Of art and piety—Pantheon!—pride of Rome!

CXLVII.

Relic of nobler days, and noblest arts!   1315
Despoiled yet perfect, with thy circle spreads
A holiness appealing to all hearts—
To art a model; and to him who treads
Rome for the sake of ages, Glory sheds
Her light through thy sole aperture; to those   1320
Who worship, here are altars for their beads;
And they who feel for genius may repose
Their eyes on honored forms, whose busts around them close.

CXLVIII.

There is a dungeon,[1] in whose dim, drear light
What do I gaze on?   Nothing: Look again!   1325
Two forms are slowly shadowed on my sight—
Two insulated phantoms of the brain:
It is not so; I see them full and plain—
An old man, and a female young and fair,
Fresh as a nursing mother, in whose vein   1330
The blood is nectar:—but what doth she there,
With her unmantled neck, and bosom white and bare?

---

[1] Byron says: "This and the three next stanzas allude to the story of the Roman daughter, which is recalled to the traveler by the site, or pretended site, of that adventure, now shown at the Church of St. Nicholas *in Carcere*." Tozer tells us that the same story of the young mother feeding her father with her own milk "is found elsewhere in various countries."

CXLIX.

Full swells the deep, pure fountain of young life,
Where *on* the heart and *from* the heart we took
Our first and sweetest nurture, when the wife,   1335
Blest into mother, in the innocent look,
Or even the piping cry of lips that brook
No pain and small suspense, a joy perceives
Man knows not, when from out its cradled nook
She sees her little bud put forth its leaves—   1340
What may the fruit be yet?   I know not—Cain was Eve's.

CL.

But here youth offers to old age the food,
The milk of his own gift: it is her sire
To whom she renders back the debt of blood
Born with her birth.   No; he shall not expire   1345
While in those warm and lovely veins the fire
Of health and holy feeling can provide
Great Nature's Nile, whose deep stream rises higher
Than Egypt's river: from that gentle side   ❧
Drink, drink and live, old man!   Heaven's realm holds no
    such tide.   1350

CLI.

The starry fable of the milky way [1]
Has not thy story's purity; it is
A constellation of a sweeter ray,
And sacred Nature triumphs more in this
Reverse of her decree, than in the abyss   1355
Where sparkle distant worlds:—Oh, holiest nurse!

[1] The fable that milk spilled from the breast of Juno produced the Milky Way.

No drop of that clear stream its way shall miss
To thy sire's heart, replenishing its source
With life, as our freed souls rejoin the universe.

CLII.

Turn to the Mole which Hadrian reared on high,[1]   1360
Imperial mimic of old Egypt's piles,[2]
Colossal copyist of deformity,
Whose traveled fantasy from the far Nile's
Enormous model, doomed the artist's toils
To build for giants, and for his vain earth,   1365
His shrunken ashes, raise this dome: How smiles
The gazer's eye with philosophic mirth,
To view the huge design which sprung from such a birth!

CLIII.

But lo! the dome[3]—the vast and wondrous dome,
To which Diana's marvel[4] was a cell—   1370
Christ's mighty shrine above his martyr's tomb!
I have beheld the Ephesian's miracle;—
Its columns strew the wilderness, and dwell
The hyena and the jackal in their shade;
I have beheld Sophia's[5] bright roofs swell   1375
Their glittering mass i' the sun, and have surveyed
Its sanctuary the while the usurping Moslem prayed;

CLIV.

But thou, of temples old, or altars new,
Standest alone, with nothing like to thee—

---

[1] Now the castle of St. Angelo, once the mausoleum of Hadrian.
[2] The pyramids.   [3] St. Peter's at Rome.
[4] The temple of Diana at Ephesus.
[5] The gilded dome of St. Sophia's, Constantinople. The church is now
a mosque.

Worthiest of God, the holy and the true.   1380
Since Zion's desolation,[1] when that He
Forsook His former city, what could be,
Of earthly structures, in His honor piled,
Of a sublimer aspect?   Majesty,
Power, Glory, Strength, and Beauty all are aisled   1385
In this eternal ark of worship undefiled.

CLV.

Enter: its grandeur overwhelms thee not;
And why?   It is not lessened; but thy mind,
Expanded by the genius of the spot,
Has grown colossal, and can only find   1390
A fit abode wherein appear enshrined
Thy hopes of immortality; and thou
Shalt one day, if found worthy, so defined,
See thy God face to face, as thou dost now
His Holy of Holies, nor be blasted by his brow.   1395

CLVI.

Thou movest, but increasing with the advance,
Like climbing some great Alp, which still doth rise,
Deceived by its gigantic elegance;
Vastness which grows, but grows to harmonize—
All musical in its immensities;   1400
Rich marbles, richer painting—shrines where flame
The lamps of gold—and haughty dome which vies
In air with Earth's chief structures, though their frame
Sits on the firm-set ground, and this the clouds must claim.

CLVII.

Thou seest not all; but piecemeal thou must break,   1405
To separate contemplation, the great whole;

---

[1] The Jewish temple at Jerusalem, destroyed by the Romans A.D. 70.

And as the ocean many bays will make
That ask the eye—so here condense thy soul
To more immediate objects, and control
Thy thoughts until thy mind hath got by heart   1410
Its eloquent proportions, and unroll
In mighty graduations, part by part,
The glory which at once upon thee did not dart,

CLVIII.

Not by its fault—but thine : Our outward sense
Is but of gradual grasp—and as it is   1415
That what we have of feeling most intense
Outstrips our faint expression ; even so this
Outshining and o'erwhelming edifice
Fools our fond gaze, and greatest of the great
Defie; at first our Nature's littleness,   1420
Till, growing with its growth, we thus dilate
Our spirits to the size of that they contemplate.

CLIX.

Then pause, and be enlightened ; there is more
In such a survey than the sating gaze
Of wonder pleased, or awe which would adore   1425
The worship of the place, or the mere praise
Of art and its great masters, who could raise
What former time, nor skill, nor thought could plan ;
The fountain of sublimity displays
Its depth, and thence may draw the mind of man   1430
Its golden sands, and learn what great conceptions can.

CLX.

Or, turning to the Vatican, go see
Laocoön's torture dignifying pain [1] —

1 The original Laocoön group is in the Vatican. (See Æneid, ii., for the story.)

A father's love and mortal's agony
With an immortal's patience blending: Vain　　　　1435
The struggle; vain, against the coiling strain
And gripe, and deepening of the dragon's grasp,
The old man's clinch; the long envenomed chain
Rivets the living links,—the enormous asp
Enforces pang on pang, and stifles gasp on gasp.　　　1440

CLXI.

Or view the lord of the unerring bow,[1]
The god of life, and poesy, and light—
The sun in human limbs arrayed, and brow
All radiant from his triumph in the fight;
The shaft hath just been shot—the arrow bright　　　1445
With an immortal's vengeance; in his eye
And nostril beautiful disdain, and might
And majesty, flash their full lightnings by,
Developing in that one glance the Deity.

CLXII.

But in his delicate form—a dream of love,　　　　1450
Shaped by some solitary nymph, whose breast
Longed for a deathless lover from above,
And maddened in that vision—are expressed
All that ideal beauty ever blessed
The mind within its most unearthly mood,　　　　1455
When each conception was a heavenly guest—
A ray of immortality—and stood
Starlike, around, until they gathered to a god!

CLXIII.

And if it be Prometheus [2] stole from heaven
The fire which we endure, it was repaid　　　　1460

---

[1] The Apollo Belvedere.
[2] Read Longfellow's poem, Prometheus, or the Poet's Forethought.

By him to whom the energy was given
Which this poetic marble hath arrayed
With an eternal glory—which, if made
By human hands, is not of human thought;
And Time himself hath hallowed it, nor laid   1465
One ringlet in the dust—nor hath it caught
A tinge of years, but breathes the flame with which 'twas
     wrought.

CLXIV.

But where is he, the Pilgrim [1] of my song,
The being who upheld it through the past?
Methinks he cometh late and tarries long.   1470
He is no more—these breathings are his last;
His wanderings done, his visions ebbing fast,
And he himself as nothing:—if he was
Aught but a fantasy, and could be classed
With forms which live and suffer—let that pass—   1475
His shadow fades away into Destruction's mass,

CLXV.

Which gathers shadow, substance, life, and all
That we inherit in its mortal shroud,
And spreads the dim and universal pall   1479
Through which all things grow phantoms; and the cloud
Between us sinks and all which ever glowed,
Till Glory's self is twilight, and displays
A melancholy halo scarce allowed
To hover on the verge of darkness; rays
Sadder than saddest night, for they distract the gaze,   1485

CLXVI.

And send us prying into the abyss,
To gather what we shall be when the frame

[1] Childe Harold, last mentioned in Canto III. Stanza LV.

10

Shall be resolved to something less than this
Its wretched essence ; and to dream of fame,
And wipe the dust from off the idle name   1490
We nevermore shall hear,—but nevermore,
Oh, happier thought! can we be made the same :
It is enough, in sooth, that *once* we bore
These fardels[1] of the heart—the heart whose sweat was gore.

CLXVII.[2]

Hark! forth from the abyss a voice proceeds,   1495
A long low distant murmur of dread sound,
Such as arises when a nation bleeds
With some deep and immedicable wound ;
Through storm and darkness yawns the rending ground,
The gulf is thick with phantoms, but the chief   1500
Seems royal still, though with her head discrowned,
And pale, but lovely, with maternal grief
She clasps a babe, to whom her breast yields no relief.

CLXVIII.

Scion of chiefs and monarchs, where art thou?
Fond hope of many nations, art thou dead?   1505
Could not the grave forget thee, and lay low
Some less majestic, less belovèd head?
In the sad midnight, while thy heart still bled,
The mother of a moment, o'er thy boy,

[1] Troubles. " Who would fardels bear," etc. (Hamlet, iii. i.).
[2] " From the thought of death the poet passes to the death of the Princess Charlotte, which happened when he was at Venice. No other event during the present century has caused so great a shock to public feeling in England ; and Byron himself, as we learn from his letters, was deeply moved by it. She was the only daughter of George IV., who at that time was prince regent, and consequently she was heiress presumptive to the British crown " (TOZER).

Death hushed that pang forever: with thee fled   1510
The present happiness and promised joy
Which filled the imperial isles so full it seemed to cloy.

CLXIX.

Peasants bring forth in safety.—Can it be,
O thou that wert so happy, so adored!
Those who weep not for kings shall weep for thee,   1515
And Freedom's heart, grown heavy, cease to hoard
Her many griefs for ONE; for she had poured
Her orisons for thee, and o'er thy head
Beheld her Iris.[1]—Thou, too, lonely lord,
And desolate consort—vainly wert thou wed!   1520
The husband of a year! the father of the dead!

CLXX.

Of sackcloth was thy wedding garment made;
Thy bridal's fruit is ashes: in the dust
The fair-haired Daughter of the Isles is laid,
The love of millions!   How we did intrust   1525
Futurity to her! and, though it must
Darken above our bones, yet fondly deemed
Our children should obey her child, and blessed
Her and her hoped-for seed, whose promise seemed   1529
Like stars to shepherds' eyes:—'twas but a meteor beamed.

CLXXI.

Woe unto us, not her; for she sleeps well:
The fickle reek of popular breath, the tongue
Of hollow counsel, the false oracle,
Which from the birth of monarchy hath rung

---

1 The rainbow, emblem of hope.

Its knell in princely ears, till the o'erstrung   1535
Nations have armed in madness, the strange fate
Which tumbles mightiest sovereigns, and hath flung
Against their blind omnipotence a weight
Within the opposing scale, which crushes soon or late,—

CLXXII.

These might have been her destiny; but no,   1540
Our hearts deny it: and so young, so fair,
Good without effort, great without a foe;
But now a bride and mother—and now *there!*
How many ties did that stern moment tear!
From thy sire's to his humblest subject's breast   1545
Is linked the electric chain of that despair,
Whose shock was as an earthquake's, and oppressed
The land which loved thee so that none could love thee best.

CLXXIII.

Lo, Nemi![1] naveled in the woody hills
So far, that the uprooting wind which tears   1550
The oak from his foundation, and which spills
The ocean o'er its boundary, and bears
Its form against the skies, reluctant spares
The oval mirror of thy glassy lake;
And calm as cherished hate, its surface wears   1555
A deep cold settled aspect naught can shake,
All coiled into itself and round, as sleeps the snake.

CLXXIV.

And near, Albano's[2] scarce divided waves
Shine from a sister valley;—and afar

[1] "The village of Nemi was near the Arician retreat of Egeria, and from the shades which embosomed the temple of Diana, has preserved to this day its distinctive appellation of The Grove. Nemi is but an evening's ride from the comfortable inn of Albano" (BYRON).   [2] A lake in the Alban Hill.

The Tiber winds, and the broad ocean laves   1560
The Latian coast where sprung the Epic war,
" Arms and the man," whose reascending star
Rose o'er an empire : —but beneath thy right
Tully reposed from Rome ;—and where yon ba.
Of girdling mountains intercepts the sight   1565
The Sabine farm was tilled, the weary bard's delight.

CLXXV.

But I forget.—My Pilgrim's shrine is won,
And he and I must part,—so let it be,—
His task and mine alike are nearly done ;
Yet once more let us look upon the sea ;   1570
The midland ocean [1] breaks on him and me,
And from the Alban Mount we now behold
Our friend of youth, that Ocean, which when we
Beheld it last by Calpe's rock [2] unfold
Those waves, we followed on till the dark Euxine rolled 1575

CLXXVI.

Upon the blue Symplegades : [3] long years—
Long, though not very many—since have done
Their work on both ; some suffering and some tears
Have left us nearly where we had begun :
Yet not in vain our mortal race hath run ;   1580
We have had our reward, and it is here,—
That we can yet feel gladdened by the sun,
And reap from earth, sea, joy almost as dear
As if there were no man to trouble what is clear.

CLXXVII.

Oh! that the Desert were my dwelling place,   1585
With one fair Spirit for my minister,

[1] The Mediterranean.   [2] Gibraltar.
[3] Two small islands at the entrance of the Black Sea from the Bosporus.

That I might all forget the human race,
And hating no one, love but only her!
Ye Elements!—in whose ennobling stir
I feel myself exalted—can ye not   1590
Accord me such a being?   Do I err
In deeming such inhabit many a spot?
Though with them to converse can rarely be our lot.

CLXXVIII.[1]

There is a pleasure in the pathless woods,
There is a rapture on the lonely shore,   1595
There is society, where none intrudes,
By the deep Sea, and music in its roar:
I love not Man the less, but Nature more,
From these our interviews, in which I steal
From all I may be, or have been before,   1600
To mingle with the Universe, and feel
What I can ne'er express, yet cannot all conceal.

CLXXIX.

Roll on, thou deep and dark blue Ocean—roll!
Ten thousand fleets sweep over thee in vain;
Man marks the earth with ruin—his control   1605
Stops with the shore; upon the watery plain
The wrecks are all thy deed, nor doth remain
A shadow of man's ravage, save his own,
When, for a moment, like a drop of rain,
He sinks into thy depths with bubbling groan,   1610
Without a grave, unknelled, uncoffined, and unknown.

CLXXX.

His steps are not upon thy paths,—thy fields
Are not a spoil for him,—thou dost arise

---

[1] " Stanzas CLXXVIII.-CLXXXIV. form a splendid passage that has long been classical " (KEENE).

And shake him from thee ; the vile strength he wields
For earth's destruction thou dost all despise,   1615
Spurning him from thy bosom to the skies,
And send'st him, shivering in thy playful spray
And howling, to his Gods, where haply lies
His petty hope in some near port or bay,
And dashest him again to earth : —there let him lay.   1620

CLXXXI.

The armaments which thunderstrike the walls
Of rock-built cities, bidding nations quake,
And monarchs tremble in their capitals,
The oak leviathans, whose huge ribs make
Their clay creator the vain title take   1625
Of lord of thee, and arbiter of war—
These are thy toys, and, as the snowy flake,
They melt into thy yeast of waves, which mar
Alike the Armada's pride or spoils of Trafalgar.

CLXXXII.

Thy shores are empires, changed in all save thee—   1630
Assyria, Greece, Rome, Carthage, what are they?
Thy waters washed them power while they were free,
And many a tyrant since ; their shores obey
The stranger, slave, or savage ; their decay
Has dried up realms to deserts : —not so thou ; —   1635
Unchangeable, save to thy wild waves' play,
Time writes no wrinkle on thine azure brow :
Such as creation's dawn beheld, thou rollest now.

CLXXXIII.

Thou glorious mirror, where the Almighty's form
Glasses itself in tempests ; in all time,—   1640
Calm or convulsed, in breeze, or gale, or storm,
Icing the pole, or in the torrid clime

Dark-heaving—boundless, endless, and sublime,
The image of eternity, the throne
Of the Invisible; even from out thy slime   1645
The monsters of the deep are made; each zone
Obeys thee; thou goest forth, dread, fathomless, alone.

CLXXXIV.

And I have loved thee, Ocean! and my joy
Of youthful sports was on thy breast to be
Borne, like thy bubbles, onward: from a boy   1650
I wantoned with thy breakers—they to me
Were a delight; and if the freshening sea
Made them a terror—'twas a pleasing fear,
For I was as it were a child of thee,
And trusted to thy billows far and near,   1655
And laid my hand upon thy mane—as I do here.

CLXXXV.

My task is done, my song hath ceased, my theme
Has died into an echo; it is fit
The spell should break of this protracted dream.
The torch shall be extinguished which hath lit   1660
My midnight lamp—and what is writ, is writ;
Would it were worthier! but I am not now
That which I have been—and my visions flit
Less palpably before me—and the glow
Which in my spirit dwelt is fluttering, faint, and low.   1665

CLXXXVI.

Farewell! a word that must be, and hath been—
A sound which makes us linger;—yet—farewell!

Ye! who have traced the Pilgrim to the scene
Which is his last, if in your memories dwell
A thought which once was his, if on ye swell   1670
A single recollection, not in vain
He wore his sandal shoon and scallop shell;
Farewell! with *him* alone may rest the pain,
If such there were—with *you*, the moral of his strain.

SONG OF THE GREEK BARD.

FROM THE THIRD CANTO OF "DON JUAN."

1.

THE isles of Greece, the isles of Greece!
   Where burning Sappho [1] loved and sung,
Where grew the arts of war and peace,
   Where Delos [2] rose, and Phœbus [2] sprung!
Eternal summer gilds them yet,   5
But all, except their sun, is set.

2.

The Scian [3] and the Teian [4] muse,
   The hero's harp, the lover's lute,
Have found the fame your shores refuse:
   Their place of birth alone is mute   10

[1] A Greek poetess who was in the zenith of her fame about B.C. 600.
"The glory of Lesbos (Mitylene) was that Sappho was its citizen, and its
chief fame centers in the fact of her celebrity." The poet Swinburne calls
Sappho
    "Love's priestess, mad with pain and joy of song,
    Song's priestess, mad with joy and pain of love."

[2] An island fabled to have been raised from the sea by Neptune for Latona,
mother of the twin children Apollo (Phœbus) and Diana, born on Delos.
 [3] Homer, born at Scio.
 [4] Anacreon, born on the isle of Teos.

To sounds which echo further west
Than your sires' " Islands of the Blest." [1]

3.

The mountains look on Marathon [2]—
And Marathon looks on the sea;
And musing there an hour alone,   15
  I dreamed that Greece might still be free;
For standing on the Persians' grave,   •
I could not deem myself a slave.

4.

A king [3] sate on the rocky brow
  Which looks o'er sea-born Salamis; [4]   20
And ships, by thousands, lay below,
  And men in nations;—all were his!
He counted them at break of day—
And when the sun set where were they?

5.

And where are they? and where art thou,   25
  My country?   On thy voiceless shore
The heroic lay is tuneless now—
  The heroic bosom beats no more!
And must thy lyre, so long divine,
Degenerate into hands like mine?   30

---

[1] " The νῆσοι μακάρων of the Greek poets were supposed to have been the
Cape Verde Islands or the Canaries " (BYRON).

[2] In Attica,—the scene of one of the world's decisive battles.   Here, in
B.C. 490, 11,000 Greeks under Miltiades defeated 100,000 Persians.   On
this and the other historic events mentioned in the poem, consult some good
Greek history.

[3] Xerxes, king of the Persians.

[4] An island of ancient Greece, opposite Athens,—the scene of the famous
victory over the Persians by the Greek fleet under Themistocles, B.C. 480.

6.

'Tis something, in the dearth of fame,
  Though linked among a fettered race,
To feel at least a patriot's shame,
  Even as I sing, suffuse my face;
For what is left the poet here?   35
For Greeks a blush—for Greece a tear.[1]

7.

Must *we* but weep o'er days more blest?
Must *we* but blush?—Our fathers bled.
Earth! render back from out thy breast
  A remnant of our Spartan dead!   40
Of the three hundred grant but three,
To make a new Thermopylæ![2]

8.

What, silent still? and silent all?
  Ah! no;—the voices of the dead
Sound like a distant torrent's fall,   45
  And answer, "Let one living head,[3]
But one arise,—we come, we come!"
'Tis but the living who are dumb.

---

[1] Byron, in Don Juan, Canto III. Stanza LXXXVII., thus refers to his Greek Bard:
  "Thus sung, or would, or could, or should have sung,
    The modern Greek, in tolerable verse;
  If not like Orpheus quite, when Greece was young,
    Yet in these times he might have done much worse:
  His strain displayed some feeling—right or wrong;
    And feeling, in a poet, is the source
  Of others' feeling; but they are such liars,
  And take all colors—like the hands of dyers."

[2] A narrow pass—the only road from northern to southern Greece, defended by the Spartan leader Leonidas against the Persians, B.C. 480.

[3] What did Byron himself do for the Greek cause?

9.

In vain—in vain : strike other chords ;
Fill high the cup with Samian [1] wine!   50
Leave battles to the Turkish hordes,
And shed the blood of Scio's [2] vine!
Hark! rising to the ignoble call—
How answers each bold Bacchanal! [3]

10.

You have the Pyrrhic [4] dance as yet ;   55
Where is the Pyrrhic phalanx gone?
Of two such lessons, why forget
The nobler and the manlier one?
You have the letters Cadmus [5] gave—
Think ye he meant them for a slave?   60

11.

Fill high the bowl with Samian wine!
We will not think of themes like these!
It made Anacreon's song divine :
He served—but served Polycrates [6]—
A tyrant ; but our masters then   65
Were still, at least, our countrymen.

[1] Of Samos, an island off the coast of Asia Minor.
[2] A city noted for its wine, situated on an island of the same name in the Ægean Sea.
[3] A devotee of Bacchus.
[4] Byron saw and described

　　　" The Pyrrhic dance so martial,
　　　To which the Levantines are very partial."

The Greeks learned the use of the phalanx and the war dance from Pyrrhus, king of Epirus.
[5] Cadmus, a Phœnician, is said to have brought the alphabet to Greece.
[6] Polycrates, tyrant of the island of Samos, in the Ægean Sea, was a patron of literature.

12.

The tyrant of the Chersonese [1]
  Was freedom's best and bravest friend;
That tyrant was Miltiades! [2]
  Oh! that the present hour would lend   70
Another despot of the kind!
Such chains as his were sure to bind.

13.

Fill high the bowl with Samian wine!
  On Suli's rock, [3] and Parga's [4] shore,
Exists the remnant of a line   75
  Such as the Doric mothers bore;
And there, perhaps, some seed is sown,
The Heracleidan [5] blood might own.

14.

Trust not for freedom to the Franks [6]—
  They have a king who buys and sells;   80
In native swords, and native ranks,
  The only hope of courage dwells:
But Turkish force, and Latin fraud,
Would break your shield, however broad. [7]

15.

Fill high the bowl with Samian wine!   85
  Our virgins dance beneath the shade—

[1] A peninsula of Greece.
[2] The leader of the Greeks at Marathon.
[3] A famous fortress in Epirus.
[4] A fortified town in Turkey.
[5] Descended from Hercules, who was of Doric origin.
[6] Inhabitants of France.
[7] Did not Turkish force, Latin fraud, and Greek cowardice break the Greek shield in 1897?

I see their glorious black eyes shine;
But gazing on each glowing maid,
My own the burning tear-drop laves,
To think such breasts must suckle slaves.   90

16.

Place me on Sunium's [1] marbled steep,
Where nothing, save the waves and I,
May hear our mutual murmurs sweep;
There, swanlike, let me sing and die:
A land of slaves shall ne'er be mine—   95
Dash down yon cup of Samian wine!

[1] Cape Sunium or Colonna, a rocky promontory. Byron alludes to some lines of Sophocles, in the tragedy of Ajax, in which a hero says : " Let me be where is the surf-beaten promontory of the sea, under the lofty hill of Sunium."

GENERAL NOTE.—The impassioned eloquence of this unique poem is wonderfully effective. As The Prisoner of Chillon is the least Byronic of the author's best poems, this may be said to be the most Byronic. Besides its supreme merit as a work of literary art, the brilliant lyric affords many historical data, and furnishes a fruitful theme not only for a lesson, but for a whole lecture, on Greece, ancient and modern, her wars, heroes, poets, and patriotic struggles, which seem destined never to end. The poem should be " committed to memory," and, what is better, " learned by heart."

DARKNESS.

I HAD a dream, which was not all a dream.
The bright sun was extinguished, and the stars
Did wander darkling in the eternal space,
Rayless, and pathless; and the icy earth
Swung blind and blackening in the moonless air;   5
Morn came and went—and came, and brought no day,
And men forgot their passions in the dread
Of this their desolation; and all hearts
Were chilled into a selfish prayer for light:
And they did live by watch fires—and the thrones,   10
The palaces of crownèd kings—the huts,
The habitations of all things which dwell,
Were burnt for beacons; cities were consumed,
And men were gathered round their blazing homes
To look once more into each other's face;   15
Happy were those who dwelt within the eye
Of the volcanoes, and their mountain torch:
A fearful hope was all the world contained;
Forests were set on fire—but hour by hour   ·
They fell and faded—and the crackling trunks   20
Extinguished with a crash—and all was black.
The brows of men by the despairing light
Wore an unearthly aspect, as by fits
The flashes fell upon them; some lay down

And hid their eyes and wept; and some did rest   25
Their chins upon their clinchèd hands, and smiled;
And others hurried to and fro, and fed
Their funeral piles with fuel, and looked up
With mad disquietude on the dull sky,
The pall of a past world; and then again   30
With curses cast them down upon the dust,
And gnashed their teeth and howled : the wild birds shrieked,
And, terrified, did flutter on the ground,
And flap their useless wings; the wildest brutes
Came tame and tremulous; and vipers crawled   35
And twined themselves among the multitude,
Hissing, but stingless—they were slain for food!
And War, which for a moment was no more,
Did glut himself again : —a meal was bought ·
With blood, and each sate sullenly apart   40
Gorging himself in gloom: no love was left;
All earth was but one thought—and that was death
Immediate and inglorious; and the pang
Of famine fed upon all entrails—men
Died, and their bones were tombless as their flesh;   45
The meager by the meager were devoured,
Even dogs assailed their masters, all save one,
And he was faithful to a corse, and kept
The birds and beasts and famished men at bay,
Till hunger clung them, or the dropping dead   50
Lured their lank jaws; himself sought out no food,
But with a piteous and perpetual moan,
And a quick desolate cry, licking the hand
Which answered not with a caress—he died.
The crowd was famished by degrees; but two   55
Of an enormous city did survive,
And they were enemies: they met beside
The dying embers of an altar place
Where had been heaped a mass of holy things

11

For an unholy usage; they raked up,   60
And shivering scraped with their cold skeleton hands
The feeble ashes, and their feeble breath
Blew for a little life, and made a flame
Which was a mockery; then they lifted up
Their eyes as it grew lighter, and beheld   65
Each other's aspects—saw, and shrieked, and died—
Even of their mutual hideousness they died,
Unknowing who he was upon whose brow
Famine had written Fiend. The world was void,
The populous and the powerful was a lump,   70
Seasonless, herbless, treeless, manless, lifeless,
A lump of death—a chaos of hard clay.
The rivers, lakes, and ocean all stood still,
And nothing stirred within their silent depths;
Ships sailorless lay rotting on the sea,   75
And their masts fell down piecemeal: as they dropped
They slept on the abyss without a surge—
The waves were dead; the tides were in their grave,
The Moon, their mistress, had expired before;
The winds were withered in the stagnant air,   80
And the clouds perished; Darkness had no need
Of aid from them—She was the Universe!

Diodati, July, 1816.

THE DESTRUCTION OF SEN-NACHERIB.[1]

I.

THE Assyrian came down like the wolf on the fold,
And his cohorts were gleaming in purple and gold;
And the sheen of their spears was like stars on the sea,
When the blue wave rolls nightly on deep Galilee.

II.

Like the leaves of the forest when Summer is green,   5
That host with their banners at sunset were seen:
Like the leaves of the forest when Autumn hath blown,
That host on the morrow lay withered and strown.

III.

For the Angel of Death[2] spread his wings on the blast,
And breathed in the face of the foe as he passed;   10
And the eyes of the sleepers waxed deadly and chill,
And their hearts but once heaved, and forever grew still!

[1] This musical lyric is a good specimen of Byron's Hebrew Melodies, of which there are twenty, a few of the most noted being those entitled Vision of Belshazzar, She Walks in Beauty, and The Wild Gazelle. Compare the poem with Thomas Moore's Sound the Loud Timbrel, a still finer Hebrew melody. Sennacherib, king of Assyria, reigned from B.C. 705 to 681.

[2] " And the Lord sent an angel, which cut off all the mighty men of valor,

163

IV.

And there lay the steed with his nostril all wide,
But through it there rolled not the breath of his pride;
And the foam of his gasping lay white on the turf,   15
And cold as the spray of the rock-beating surf.

V.

And there lay the rider distorted and pale,
With the dew on his brow, and the rust on his mail:
And the tents were all silent, the banners alone,
The lances unlifted, the trumpet unblown.   20

VI.

And the widows of Ashur are loud in their wail,
And the idols are broke in the temple of Baal;
And the might of the Gentile, unsmote by the sword,
Hath melted like snow in the glance of the Lord!

and the leaders and captains in the camp of the king of Assyria. So he returned with shame of face to his own land" (II. Chronicles xxxii. 21).

TO THOMAS MOORE.[1]

I.

My boat is on the shore,
   And my bark is on the sea;
But, before I go, Tom Moore,
   Here's a double health to thee!

II.

Here's a sigh to those who love me,   5
   And a smile to those who hate;
And, whatever sky's above me,
   Here's a heart for every fate.

III.

Though the ocean roar around me,
   Yet it still shall bear me on;   10
Though a desert should surround me,
   It hath springs that may be won.

[1] Thomas Moore, Byron's friend and biographer, an Irish poet (born 1779, died 1852), author of many beautiful songs.

IV.

Were't the last drop in the well,
  As I gasped upon the brink,
Ere my fainting spirit fell,   15
  'Tis to thee that I would drink.

V.

With that water, as this wine,
  The libation I would pour
Should be—peace with thine and mine,
  And a health to thee, Tom Moore.   20

July, 1817.

WHEN COLDNESS WRAPS THIS SUFFERING CLAY.[1]

I.

WHEN coldness wraps this suffering clay,
   Ah! whither strays the immortal mind?
It cannot die, it cannot stay,
   But leaves its darkened dust behind.
Then, unembodied, doth it trace   5
   By steps each planet's heavenly way?   .
Or fill at once the realms of space,
   A thing of eyes, that all survey?

II.

Eternal, boundless, undecayed,
   A thought unseen, but seeing all,   10
All, all in earth or skies displayed,
   Shall it survey, shall it recall:
Each fainter trace that memory holds
   So darkly of departed years,
In one broad glance the soul beholds,   15
   And all that was at once appears.

[1] This solemn strain of meditative verse reveals Byron's feeling in regard to death and the immortality of the soul.

III.

Before Creation peopled earth,
  Its eye shall roll through chaos back ;
And where the furthest heaven had birth,
  The spirit trace its rising track.   20
And where the future mars or makes,
  Its glance dilate o'er all to be,
While sun is quenched or system breaks,
  Fixed in its own eternity.

IV.

Above or Love, Hope, Hate, or Fear,   25
  It lives all passionless and pure :
An age shall fleet like earthly year;
  Its years as moments shall endure.
Away, away, without a wing,
  O'er all, through all, its thought shall fly,   30
A nameless and eternal thing,
  Forgetting what it was to die.

ON THIS DAY I COMPLETE MY THIRTY-SIXTH YEAR.[1]

<hr>

MISSOLONGHI, January 22, 1824.

'TIS time this heart should be unmoved,
  Since others it hath ceased to move:
Yet, though I cannot be beloved,
    Still let me love!

My days are in the yellow leaf;   5
  The flowers and fruits of love are gone;
The worm, the canker, and the grief
    Are mine alone!

The fire that on my bosom preys
  Is lone as some volcanic isle;   10
No torch is kindled at its blaze—
    A funeral pile.

The hope, the fear, the jealous care,
  The exalted portion of the pain
And power of love, I cannot share,   15
    But wear the chain.

[1] Byron died April 19, 1824, about three months after writing this prophetic poem. The last stanza is a fit epitaph for the brave poet.

169

But 'tis not *thus*—and 'tis not *here*—
 Such thoughts should shake my soul, nor *now*,
Where glory decks the hero's bier,
  Or binds his brow.   20

The sword, the banner, and the field,
 Glory and Greece, around me see!
The Spartan, borne upon his shield,
  Was not more free.

Awake! (not Greece—she *is* awake!) 25
 Awake, my spirit! Think through *whom*
Thy lifeblood tracks its parent lake,
  And then strike home!

Tread those reviving passions down,
 Unworthy manhood!—unto thee 30
Indifferent should the smile or frown
  Of beauty be.

If thou regrett'st thy youth, *why live?*
 The land of honorable death
Is here:—up to the field, and give 35
  Away thy breath!

Seek out—less often sought than found—
 A soldier's grave, for thee the best;
Then look around, and choose thy ground,
  And take thy rest.   40

www.ingramcontent.com/pod-product-compliance
Lightning Source LLC
Chambersburg PA
CBHW031118020726
47495CB00007B/2248

* 9 7 8 3 3 3 7 4 8 3 6 3 0 *